He'd had the dream again,

Blake knew, and as he became aware of his cheek nestled into soft female breasts, he thought he must surely be having another. Then he recognized the special scent that belonged to Jenny.

How had this happened?

He'd fallen asleep on the couch, he realized, and the dream had sucked him in. He remembered reliving the crash that always ended in black oblivion and fiery pain. But he'd never before awakened to such a wonder as this.

Jenny was so lovely, and she was so near, and Blake experienced a surge of desire he hadn't felt in a very long time. His throat constricted with the need to taste her, to lose himself in her softness.

But a shadowy memory raced in. He was a strong, attractive man no longer. He hadn't the right....

Dear Reader,

Welcome to Silhouette **Special Edition** . . . welcome to romance. Each month, Silhouette **Special Edition** publishes six novels with you in mind—stories of love and life, tales that you can identify with—romance with that little "something special" added in.

And this month has some wonderful stories in store for you. Lindsay McKenna's *One Man's War* continues her saga that is set in Vietnam during the sixties— MOMENTS OF GLORY. These powerful tales will capture you from the first page until the last! And we have an exciting debut this month—Debbie Macomber begins her new series, THOSE MANNING MEN. Don't miss the first book—*Marriage of Inconvenience*— Rich and Jamie's story.

Rounding out March are more stories by some of your favorite authors: Mary Curtis, Erica Spindler, Pamela Toth and Pat Warren. It's a wonderful month for love!

In each Silhouette **Special Edition** novel, we're dedicated to bringing you the romances that you dream about—stories that will delight as well as bring a tear to the eye. And that's what Silhouette **Special Edition** is all about—special books by special authors for special readers!

I hope you enjoy this book and all of the stories to come!

Sincerely,

Tara Gavin
Senior Editor
Silhouette Books

PAT WARREN
Under Sunny Skies

Silhouette Special Edition

Published by Silhouette Books New York

America's Publisher of Contemporary Romance

To Mary Clare Kersten, my editor,
who makes me strive to reach for that better book

SILHOUETTE BOOKS
300 East 42nd St., New York, N.Y. 10017

UNDER SUNNY SKIES

Copyright © 1992 by Pat Warren

ISBN: 0-373-09731-X

First Silhouette Books printing March 1992

All the characters in this book have no existence outside the
imagination of the author and have no relation whatsoever to
anyone bearing the same name or names. They are not even
distantly inspired by any individual known or unknown to the
author, and all incidents are pure invention.

®: Trademark used under license and registered in the United
States Patent and Trademark Office and in other countries.

Printed in the U.S.A.

PAT WARREN,

mother of four, lives in Arizona with her travel-agent husband and a lazy white cat. She's a former newspaper columnist whose lifetime dream was to become a novelist. A strong romantic streak, a sense of humor and a keen interest in developing relationships led her to try romance novels, with which she feels very much at home.

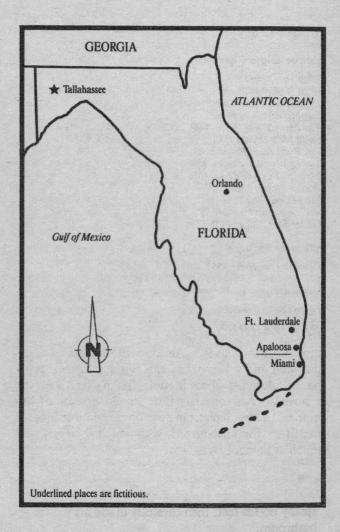

GEORGIA

★ Tallahassee

ATLANTIC OCEAN

Orlando •

FLORIDA

Gulf of Mexico

N

Ft. Lauderdale •

Apaloosa •

Miami •

Underlined places are fictitious.

Chapter One

The pain woke him, as it so often did. Blake Hanley eased his aching leg over the side of the bed and sat up. Through the slanted blinds on the high window he could see the morning sky just beginning to lighten. Rubbing his left knee, he knew there would be no more sleep for him for a while. He could take a couple of the pain pills that were on his nightstand, but he hated the floaty feeling that accompanied the numbing. He only took them when he was truly desperate.

No, he would force away the stiffness, grit his teeth against the pain and go for one of his hobbling walks. Bracing himself with clenched fists on the mattress, he pushed his lanky frame to a standing position. He stood there for a long moment until he was almost steady on his feet, then carefully made his way to the bathroom.

Minutes later, dressed in khaki cotton pants and a white T-shirt, Blake walked to the kitchen and poured himself a tall glass of orange juice. Sweat beaded his forehead from the strain of this simple morning ritual, and he frowned in annoyance as he drank.

Time, the doctors had all told him. Time would ease his movements and eventually erase his pain. He'd clung to that fragile hope.

Be patient, they'd advised as they'd stood looking down at him in his hospital bed, all of them strong and healthy and physically fit. Eighteen months later— eighteen months filled with seven operations on his nearly shattered left leg, plus skin grafts to his badly burned face—and he still had difficulty getting around. One side of his face hadn't yet healed. Day and night he was plagued by varying degrees of pain. And he was fresh out of patience.

Gingerly he touched the gauze that covered his left cheek from below his eye to just under his chin. He would apply fresh salve and change the bandage when he returned, he decided as he stepped outside. Exercise would help his weakened leg, the doctors had said, provided he could endure the discomfort. Blake would endure, he'd vowed.

He thrust his feet into the boat shoes he kept on the back porch and grabbed the carved walking stick with the brass handle that he was rarely without. Using it to steady himself, he moved down the steps, inhaling the salty air from the sea. Yes, his decision to move temporarily to this small Florida coastal town had been the right one, Blake thought as he crossed the small patch of grass and headed for the beach.

His progress was slow, but even so he reached the damp sand in minutes. The sun was just inching up over the horizon, turning the sky into misty shades of orange and blue. Gray sea gulls dipped low, then rose high in flight. He'd always wanted to live by the ocean, Blake recalled as he stopped to stare out at the steady waves rolling endlessly onto the shore. He hadn't dreamed he would have the opportunity so soon, or that he'd wind up living alone in an isolated cottage.

Turning, he gazed back at the house that was now his home. Fashioned of beige stucco, it sat on a small rise surrounded by thick vegetation—shrubs, vivid poinsettia bushes, squatty palms and cypress trees with Spanish moss roping. The garden bordering the grassy area was overgrown, and beyond that the lawn sloped into a dense woods. All of it seemed designed to protect the privacy of the cabin's occupant. And privacy was exactly what Blake was seeking.

Shifting direction, he started down the secluded stretch of beach, gradually putting more weight on his bad leg with each step. Hearing a sound in the distance, he raised his pale gray eyes. The plane was high in the sky, a silver speck as it climbed into the fluffy white clouds. About twenty thousand feet, Blake estimated, aiming for a cruising altitude of around thirty most likely. With a pang of envy he watched the commercial liner disappear from sight.

Never again would he be at the controls of a plane. Blake swallowed a hard lump of regret. In eighteen months he'd racked up a pile of regrets, but being unable to fly again was perhaps the worst. To never again feel that freedom, that exhilaration, that oneness with the universe that only flying could give him—that had to be the cruelest adjustment. He could endure any amount of pain for any length of time, if only he could fly again.

But it was not to be. Suddenly destiny had taken a decidedly downward swing. The all-American boy was grounded for good.

Thrusting the cane deeply into the uneven sand, Blake walked on, his vision slightly blurred. He'd always hated pity, self or otherwise. Even after the accident and the dismal prognosis, he'd fought against feeling sorry for himself. Life was always worth living—that was what the priest who'd counseled him at the hospital had said. Are you so sure, Father? Blake silently asked as he gazed up at the spot where he'd last seen the plane.

Maybe if he hadn't lost so much he'd agree. Maybe if he hadn't been known as the wonder boy, the handsome only child of wealthy parents who'd doted on him. Maybe if he hadn't been a superachiever—a straight-A student, the star quarterback at the University of Michigan, the fly-boy who'd joined the air force and distinguished himself on three separate foreign tours of duty, then returned a captain with a chestful of citations.

Arriving at the smooth rock formation where he usually rested, Blake eased down on the flattened end and stretched out his stiff leg. For once scarcely aware of his movements, his mind lost in his memories, he rubbed at the knee that at age thirty-two was already developing arthritis from so much punishment. He'd had it all once, Blake remembered as he scanned the horizon thoughtfully. Had it, and hadn't realized how lucky he'd been.

Perhaps the fates had decided that things had always come too easily to Blake Hanley and it was time to give his chain a good yank. Studying had been a breeze, flying had seemed as natural as breathing, and always the prettiest girls had flocked around him. He'd had money, looks, charm and the joy of doing the two things he loved most: flying and teaching. Then, in a moment, everything had changed.

It had started out as a simple training mission. Blake at the controls, the student pilot seated to his right. Shortly after takeoff something had gone wrong and they were suddenly in a dive. He'd acted purely on instinct and training, the details still a hazy memory. Later, after the crash, he had learned that he'd managed to direct the plane to an empty field, narrowly missing a nearby housing development. They'd called him a hero.

Blake hadn't felt like a hero. At Brooks Medical Center in San Antonio where they'd flown him after emergency treatment, he'd been out of it for weeks, his left leg nearly shattered and one side of his face badly burned. The pain had been beyond belief, the effect of the drugs debilitating. When he came out of the fog and was told his leg might never be normal again and that his face, despite every effort, would be badly scarred, he'd had to accept that his career was over, his dreams ended.

But there had been more.

Dealing with the sorrow of his parents had been almost as difficult as enduring his own pain. His friends had come to visit, trying valiantly to hide their pity, walking away with ill-concealed relief. Blake had turned inward then, refusing to see anyone, not wanting to talk, wanting instead to die.

After a year they'd sent him home to his parents' house, where he'd stayed in his darkened bedroom, unwilling to communicate even with those who loved him. Regularly he'd returned to Brooks for operations on his leg and for skin grafts, then back home to try to heal. Six months of that and he'd had it. He simply couldn't take any more.

Major Frank Ambrose, the surgeon in charge of his case, had been the only man able to penetrate the silent wall Blake had erected. As a doctor, he knew that Blake needed more reconstructive surgery. But he was also perceptive enough to know that a doctor has to heal more than just the body, that the man Blake was inside had been damaged, as well.

Major Ambrose had approached Blake with a proposal. His brother, Chet Ambrose, was a doctor in the coastal town of Apaloosa, Florida, a respected practitioner who in his thirty-year career had had vast and varied experience. The major had suggested turning Blake over to his brother's care for a while—checking with him regularly, letting Blake heal in his own time in his own way. Chet's wife even knew of a cottage by the sea for rent. Then, when he felt more like himself, Blake could return for more reconstructive surgery. Blake had grabbed the chance.

Though his family had protested vigorously, Blake had packed his clothes, books and records into his black Mustang and set out for Florida. He'd settled in two weeks ago, feeling better than he had in months. The pain was still present, as was the frustration over his limitations. But he was away from the hospital with its antiseptic smells and endless routine. And away from the pitying glances, the revulsion in the eyes of some, the constant concern and fussing of his folks.

With no small effort Blake struggled to his feet and braced himself with his cane, then set out for the walk back. He'd found Dr. Chet Ambrose to be as compassionate as his brother. The small hospital with which the doctor was affiliated was only twenty miles away in case Blake ran into problems. Chet had given him a generous supply of antibiotic ointment and bandages to keep on his face to prevent infection and had told him to rest and regroup. And to keep exercising his leg. Walking somewhat stiffly, Blake acknowledged that his knee felt better than when he'd awakened.

One day at a time, the Ambrose brothers had told him, and he was trying. A man needed time to adjust to all his dreams being shattered, to find a purpose in his life again. Most days Blake doubted he'd ever feel whole and confident again. But at least he was alone and away from the prying eyes and unrelenting sympathy. And alone he wanted to remain.

Carefully maneuvering around a large piece of driftwood, Blake stopped to gaze up at the sky. The mist had cleared and there, still shining, was the morning star, seemingly reluctant for the night to end. Barely visible, it twinkled encouragingly. He decided to take it as an omen of good weather ahead.

He stood there enjoying a summer wind ruffling his shaggy hair. He hadn't had a haircut in six weeks—he who had sported the trim air force cut for years. What difference did neat hair make? he asked himself. Only Dr. Ambrose ever came by. Remembering something, Blake frowned.

Someone else was coming by today, thanks to Chet's well-intentioned interference. Last week, when the good doctor stopped by for a routine check on his patient, he'd quietly looked around the small cottage. There were mounds of dishes piled in the sink, dirty clothes stacked by the laundry room—all in all, the place was in need of a good cleaning. Blake had explained that he hadn't felt up to the small chores and hated going into town to shop. It hadn't been necessary to explain how he dreaded the curious eyes that followed him everywhere.

Dr. Ambrose had insisted that Blake hire a housekeeper, recommending his own, a quiet woman who would stay out of Blake's way. Caught between a rock and a hard place, Blake had finally agreed; he knew his energy was still limited. Chet was to let him know if Moira Ryan could handle more work and, if so, bring her over this afternoon to meet him. If they got on and he hired her, Blake had decided, he'd stay in the yard while she was around. He hoped she worked quickly and was shockproof. He'd also decided that if she hovered or stared, he'd send her packing within the hour.

As he started to walk again, he heard a yipping sound and turned to gaze down the beach. A small gray dog was running in playful circles around a young woman. Blake paused to watch, realizing she thought herself alone as she whirled about, gently teasing the puppy. Gulls darted between them, several landing near the woman, their heads cocked at her antics. She was barefoot, wearing only a long, shapeless dress that hung on her slender figure, the skirt swirling around her slim legs. Her long brown hair was picked up by the breeze and tossed about her face. She laughed as she brushed it back.

She was lovely, uninhibited, natural. The sound of her laughter was musical, charming him. Yet he stepped back into the shadow of a stubby palm tree, not wanting to be seen. Bending, she picked up a piece of driftwood and sent it sailing in a high arc. The dog barked once, then raced after the stick, obviously delighted at the new game. Again the woman laughed, chasing after him.

In two weeks he'd never run into another soul on his early-morning walks along this shoreline. The nearest house was half a mile away. Of course, he didn't have exclusive rights to the beach, yet he regretted losing his privacy. For another few minutes he stood watching her graceful movements, feeling like an interloper.

There was a time when he'd have approached such a lovely woman, struck up a conversation, gotten to know her. Blake's throat tightened as he realized that this woman would probably turn and run from him if she saw his disfigured face up close. He turned and began walking back, his steps suddenly heavy. Perhaps he would take a pill, just one. A man could live day after day with just so much pain.

Jenny Starbuck sat at her aunt's kitchen table, her blue eyes softening with compassion as she listened to Dr. Ambrose speak of the man who'd recently rented the Weber Cottage a mile down the road.

"I've treated a lot of injured and sick people," Chet Ambrose went on, "and from what I've seen, there's no pain more excruciating than a serious burn. Then there's the skin grafts, and always the danger of infection." Ambrose ran his fingers along his neat beard. "From what my brother tells me, Blake Hanley is one of the bravest men he's ever come across."

"The poor man," Moira Ryan said, her soft Irish voice filled with sympathy. "It's a heavy load he's carrying."

"But why did he leave his family in Michigan and come so far?" Jenny asked.

Dr. Ambrose smiled gently at Moira's niece. "Sometimes our relatives love us, but don't understand us, or our needs. Do you remember, years ago, what it was like living with your father and your stepmother?"

Jenny felt the quick flash of pain that always accompanied thoughts of her father and the cold woman he'd married after her own mother died. "Yes, I remember."

"Blake has to deal with something similar. His folks care about him, yet they can't seem to hide their disappointment at the change his accident has made in his life. They had such high hopes for their only son."

Jenny shook back her long hair, understanding perfectly. She, too, had felt a parent's disappointment—a father's. Her mother had understood, but not Lucius Starbuck. He had let his daughter go rather than fight his second wife, who'd wanted no part of raising a child she thought difficult at best. If it hadn't been for her Aunt Moira's intervention...Jenny shuddered to think what might have happened to her. "Maybe one day his folks will come around," she offered, clinging to the hope she also held for herself.

Dr. Ambrose looked doubtful as he turned back to Moira. "So the reason I came was to ask if you could spare a couple of days a week to help him out. Blake's still recovering. He has difficulty walking and very little energy. He needs a housekeeper who will clean for him, do his wash and perhaps a little cooking. What do you say, Moira?"

Moira's round Irish face registered regret. "Ah, Doctor, you know I'd do it if I could. But with summer vacations at the library, I'm putting in four days there a week. Along with the two I spend cleaning your house, it's only the Sabbath I've left to see to my own needs." She touched his hand in apology. "I'm so sorry."

"Not to worry," Dr. Ambrose answered as he stood, letting out a disappointed sigh. "I'll inquire around and find someone else, I'm sure."

"I'll do it," Jenny said, and nearly laughed out loud when both Moira and Dr. Ambrose turned to her with identical surprised looks.

"Are you sure you want to, lass?" Moira asked. "The house is small but hasn't seen a woman's touch in months, standing vacant as it has since last Christmas."

"I'm not afraid of hard work, Aunt Moira."

"But what about your job with Dr. Swain at his vet clinic?"

"He only needs me twice a week." Jenny sent Moira an imploring smile, the one she knew usually made her aunt say yes to most any request. "Please. I need more to do and this man needs someone."

All her life Jenny had been unable to resist a creature in need, which was why she'd been drawn to work at the veterinarian clinic. She'd also been a volunteer at a nearby nursing home, visiting with the patients, rubbing their backs, pushing their wheelchairs around the grounds. From the minute the doctor had started telling them about Blake Hanley, she'd felt the same overpowering desire to reach out, to try to help someone in need.

Jenny looked up at Dr. Ambrose's thoughtful expression. She knew that the doctor's wife wouldn't be pleased if her husband asked Aunt Moira to give up her days working at the Ambrose home in order to help out at the cottage. She also knew the doctor was a busy man and probably didn't know where else to look for a woman to assist Blake Hanley. He'd known Jenny and her aunt since they'd moved to Apaloosa fifteen years ago, and he trusted them both, knew they were honest and hardworking. Yet she could see that he had some misgivings.

"Jenny, I appreciate your offer," Dr. Ambrose said, "but there's something you should consider. Captain Hanley has to adjust not only to his physical injuries but to the upheaval of his whole life. He's a pilot who can no longer fly, a very independent man who now has to depend on others. He's also a proud man who's disfigured and very self-conscious, which tends to make him moody. He's apt to be edgy and short-tempered with you."

Jenny shook her head, dismissing the doctor's warning. "He's hurting inside. That's why he's like that. I understand. I've had to make some difficult adjustments myself, and I remember how it can tear you apart if you let it. I also know what it's like to be around people who judge and criticize you. Please let me try to help him."

Moira appeared convinced. "She has a way with people, Doctor, and that's a fact. And her sunny disposition might be good for the poor man."

At last Dr. Ambrose nodded. "Okay, Jenny. Let me go discuss this with Blake, and if it's all right with him, I'll come back for you."

"Oh, you needn't bother, Doctor," Jenny said, rising. "It's only a mile's walk." She studied her watch. "It's nearly noon. I'll just spoon a bowl of the stew that's cooking, and there's apple pie freshly baked this morning. Do you think he'd like that?"

"I've no doubt he would. I think he's been living mostly on bologna sandwiches and hot dogs." Chet Ambrose moved toward the door. "You're sure you don't want me to come back to drive you?"

Jenny shook her head. "It's a beautiful day. If he doesn't wish to hire me, I'll just leave his dinner and come home. I love to walk."

Moira pushed open the screen door for him. "Aye, she's up at dawn and walking every morning with Rafferty."

At the mention of his name, the gray pup ran up onto the porch, his small body shaking in excitement as he went to Jenny and begged for the petting he knew was coming. She didn't disappoint him, bending down to ruffle his wiry fur.

"I'll wait for you at the cottage, Jenny," Dr. Ambrose said, getting into his car.

Humming, she went back inside and reached into the high cupboard for the picnic basket. Another job was just what she needed—someone to care for, a purpose to her days.

"You're sure about this, lass?" Her aunt stepped to the counter to help Jenny pack the basket. Moira's small hand flew to the coiled braids at the nape of her neck, and she fussed with the pins nervously.

Jenny stopped and turned to face her. At forty-eight there wasn't a gray hair in her aunt's rich auburn hair, and her blue eyes were as sharp as ever. Moira was only a shade over five feet, causing Jenny, who was half a foot taller, to feel oddly protective. It was her aunt's sweet smile that was her best feature, yet now Moira was frowning.

"I thought you agreed that I could be good for him."

Moira narrowed her gaze. "Aye, lass, that I did. It's just that we haven't met this captain, and he'll not be leaving the house while you'll be working there."

"Aunt Moira, he's injured and quite withdrawn, as we've just heard. Surely, if there was any real danger, Dr. Ambrose wouldn't have agreed to let me work for the man." She watched her aunt look heavenward, as if asking Jenny's dead mother what she would do in her shoes, something she did quite often. Obviously Moira needed more reassurance. "I am twenty-five, you'll recall, and not exactly uninformed."

"Wasn't I the one who explained the ways of men and women to you years ago? And the television showed you more than was decent to see. But you've known so few men, lass. Only your father and Dr. Ambrose and, of course, Dr. Swain, though he's well into his sixties." Moira reached up to stroke Jenny's cheek. "Younger men are different."

Growing impatient with her aunt's second thoughts, Jenny leaned down and hugged her. "You worry too much. I'll be fine."

"I suppose you're right." Moira glanced at the clock. "I've got to be off to the library. Lock up when you leave now, won't you, lass?"

Jenny smiled at the reminder. "Don't I always?"

"Be careful and don't be late."

Watching her leave, Jenny wrinkled her brow as she placed the covered container in the basket. Moira was worried the captain would be attracted to her. That was a needless concern, Jenny thought. She had long felt she was plain and of little interest to men.

She'd accepted it and resigned herself to the single life, such as the one her aunt lived, never marrying. She certainly wasn't unhappy, and if occasionally she longed for someone of her own who would care deeply for her alone, she'd learned to push that thought aside as unattainable. Though it was the nature of people to pine for things that could not be, Jenny refused to waste her time on foolish whims.

Adding a generous slice of pie, she covered the meal with one of her aunt's hand-embroidered Irish linen tea towels. Moira had so few things left from her years in Ireland that she cherished each one. Perhaps Captain Hanley would appreciate such a rare thing of beauty.

In the bathroom Jenny checked her appearance in the mirror. The loose-fitting robin's egg blue dress was one of her favorites and she decided not to change. Quickly she ran a comb through her long hair and stepped into white sandals.

Finding her keys, she grabbed the basket and opened the door. Rafferty came bounding over, dancing around her legs. "Yes, yes, you want to go along. But we don't know if the captain likes dogs. Perhaps the next time." Giving his head an affectionate pat, she scooted Rafferty inside and locked the door.

The sun was almost directly overhead, the sky a clear blue with only a few wispy clouds. The salty air from the sea tickled her nose. Through the palm trees she watched a graceful pelican glide to a landing on the damp sand. It was the kind of day that made you feel glad to be alive.

The thought sobered Jenny. Chances were, the wounded man in the cottage wasn't yet thinking he was glad to be alive. Though it was a long while ago, she well remembered feeling the same once. Maybe she could make a difference, Jenny thought hopefully as she walked along the side of the road.

Blake Hanley frowned as he rolled the silver ball in his left hand, flexing his fingers. His hand and arm hadn't been badly burned, and the few grafts necessary had taken well, but the taut skin needed mild exercise from time to time to keep it resilient. There was no longer any pain in this area, so that wasn't what had caused his frown. It was the news his doctor had brought him.

His housekeeper was unavailable, Chet Ambrose had said, but her niece would fill in. Blake had listened quietly to the young woman's background and had felt the tension build. Long before Chet finished, he'd arrived at his decision.

"Thanks for trying, but I don't want some young woman hanging around the house. I'll manage just fine without help."

Chet took a deep breath, as if reaching for patience. "Jenny Starbuck isn't just any young woman, Blake. She's very efficient and wouldn't be *hanging around.* She'd wash and clean, put a casserole in the oven and be on her way. I vouch for her honesty and her capabilities."

Blake leaned back in his chair and propped his leg on the ottoman. As usual when they talked, he kept his left side facing away from even his doctor. A year and a half and he was still hiding his disfigurement, he realized, as if doing so would make the scarred flesh disappear. With a disgusted sigh he squeezed the silver ball.

In his two weeks here he'd come to trust Chet Ambrose, even to confide in him, which was why he was surprised at how obtuse the man was being today. "I don't doubt your word. It's just that I came here to be alone. I don't want *anyone* around."

"You wouldn't have any trouble with Jenny," the doctor went on carefully. "She's very kind."

"Kind?" Blake let out a bitter laugh. "You mean she wouldn't scream at the sight of me. She'd just pity me." With an oath he rose to his feet unsteadily. "Damn it, Chet, you're a doctor, but you're also a man. Can't you see that I don't want a woman to stare at me with a look of sick revulsion on her face, then have to watch her struggle to hide her feelings?" One had been quite enough; he still wasn't over the hurt inflicted by her, he thought, muttering another oath.

Angrily Blake crossed the room and dropped the silver ball into a glass ashtray with a noisy thud. Why couldn't everyone just leave him the hell alone?

Chet Ambrose's expression was unreadable as he rose and dug into his pocket for his keys. "Fine. I'll ask around, see if I can find a seventy-year-old woman with a wart on the end of her nose who gets her kicks out of cleaning up after a young man who enjoys sitting around feeling sorry for himself."

Standing nearly a foot taller than the diminutive doctor, Blake's hands curled into fists. "Now look here..." Two brisk knocks on the door stopped his next words. Annoyed, he looked at Chet expectantly.

"I had to stop on the way here to check on an elderly housebound patient," Dr. Ambrose explained. "The visit took longer than I'd planned. Jenny said she'd walk over, but I thought that you and I would have plenty of time to talk before she arrived."

Seeking refuge, Blake moved into the shadowed doorway of his bedroom. "Tell her you made a mistake and that I won't be needing her."

Noticeably irritated, Chet frowned. "Blake, be reasonable. She's come all this way, expecting at least an afternoon's work. The house really needs a cleaning. She's even brought your dinner."

His sense of fair play fought with the need to protect his privacy at all costs. Years of strict training and respect for rules won, and he sighed as he opened the bedroom door. "All right, but tell her to go about her business and not disturb me. I'm going to take a nap." Moving inside, he closed the door.

Blake paced to the far side of the room, then back, feeling trapped. The house was old, but the walls weren't very thick. At the door he leaned close, listening. The voices were muffled, yet he could make out the words.

"I believe you'll find all the cleaning supplies in the pantry closet, Jenny," Dr. Ambrose was saying. "The laundry room is off the kitchen, as well. Captain Hanley is resting, so you'd best leave him be."

"I understand. I'll put his dinner to warm in the oven when I go."

Blake cocked his head. Her voice was soft, with the slightest trace of an Irish brogue, not the Southern accent he'd been expecting. He recalled that Chet had said both the girl and her aunt had been born in Ireland, but had been in the States for many years.

"I'll see about your pay later when Blake's feeling better," Dr. Ambrose said. "As I told you earlier, he's not comfortable having someone around, so I'm not sure when he'll need you again."

"It's all right, Doctor. I'll finish and be gone."

"Thanks, Jenny."

Blake heard the door close and footsteps on the front porch, then a car starting. Straining, he listened, but could hear nothing else. Where was she and what was she doing? Finally he heard water running in the bathroom. So she was starting in there. Good. He hoped she was a fast worker. He badly wanted his peace and solitude back.

Moving to the bed, he lay down gingerly, mindful that his knee was throbbing again. Probably because he'd been holding himself so rigidly, tension caused the muscles to spasm. He glanced at the pill bottle longingly, wishing for several hours of oblivion. Then when he awoke, she would be gone and he'd be alone again.

But, no, he didn't want to be fuzzy-headed while someone else was in the house. Instead, he rubbed his aching knee and closed his eyes, willing himself to sleep.

But sleep wouldn't come. After half an hour, he gave up and went back to the door to listen. The water had stopped running in the bath. Now he heard humming in the living room just outside his door, and the occasional shifting of items. She must be dusting, he decided as he heard the piano keys sound in discord. The tune she hummed seemed vaguely familiar, yet he couldn't recall the title.

Feeling like a prisoner in his own home, Blake walked to the chair by the window and sat down to read. His concentration was poor as his mind kept returning to the other rooms and the slight movements he heard. Damn, why had he agreed to even an afternoon of this torture?

After a while, he dozed off, the book sliding from his hands. When he awoke, it was to a silent house. Rising stiffly, he saw that it was past six. She must have finished and left. Cautiously he listened for several minutes at the door. Not a sound. He simply couldn't stay in his bedroom forever. Nervously he opened the door.

The living room was empty and smelled of furniture polish. It looked neat and orderly. Blake peeked into the bath and saw that it, too, was shiny clean. Well, at least the girl knew her business. An enticing aroma drew him into the kitchen.

Opening the oven, he discovered a covered dish of simmering stew. On the counter was a pan of hot rolls. His mouth began to water. Lord, but it had been a long while since he'd had a decent meal. Blake opened the cupboard and reached for a plate.

"There you are, Captain," Jenny said, backing out of the pantry closet. "Did you have a good nap?"

Blake almost dropped the dish as he swiveled about, instinctively turning so that his left side was away from the sound of her voice. He drew in a stunned breath. The girl from the beach stood there, wearing the same sky-blue dress, her long brown hair falling past her shoulders. "I thought you'd gone," he said, caught totally off guard.

She moved closer and held out her hand, smiling at him timidly. "I'm Jenny Starbuck. It's good of you to let me work for you. I've been needing a job."

He had no choice but to shake her hand, finding her skin soft yet with a strength that surprised him. He felt his stomach muscles tighten as he looked into the bluest eyes he'd ever seen. Searching their depths, he saw an unexpected shyness. "Blake Hanley," he said, feeling nonplussed.

She retrieved her hand, her eyes not leaving his. "I've nearly finished for the day, but I'm having trouble getting at your vacuum. Someone's hung it on a high hook in the closet and I can't lift it down."

Realizing he still held the plate, he set it on the counter. "It's all right. You needn't vacuum."

"Oh, but the living room needs it badly. It won't take long. I couldn't take your money without doing a thorough job."

Infuriatingly stubborn, he decided. He supposed the quickest way to get her to leave was to accommodate her. Keeping his left side averted, he maneuvered around her, tensing as he tried not to limp in front of her.

In the closet he spotted the vacuum and heaved it up and off the hook. It was an old machine, heavy as hell. Small wonder she hadn't been able to take it down. Rolling it out to her, it occurred to Blake that no one had expected him to lift anything heavier than a pillow in far too long. It made him feel good just being asked.

"Thank you," Jenny said as she stretched to put away the last of the dishes she'd washed and dried. "These cupboards are truly high."

Blake watched her breasts push against the thin cotton of her dress, and his imagination peeled away the fabric. He felt his body's reaction, reminding him that for too long he'd been without the softness of a woman. The thought did nothing to improve his mood. "I'll be out on the porch while you finish," he said somewhat gruffly as he let the screen door slam behind him.

Sitting down heavily in an old maple rocker, he ran a shaky hand over his unshaven chin. He supposed he should shave more often, though he had to use great care around the burned skin. Looking down at his wrinkled khaki pants, he thought he could also take more interest in his appearance and... wait!

What on earth was he doing? Just because he'd been in there with a woman—close enough to touch her—didn't mean he could, so who was he thinking to impress? She would turn from him if she saw what was under the bandage covering his left cheek or the surgery scars crisscrossing his leg. She was a woman who'd come here to clean—nothing more, nothing less—and she hadn't the slightest interest in him as a man.

Blake heard the vacuum humming in the living room and inhaled the aroma of stew and warm rolls drifting through the screen. At least he'd have a good meal out of today's misery. And by the next time the little house needed cleaning, he'd be up to handling the work himself. Impatiently he settled back to wait for her to leave.

"I hope you like Irish stew," Jenny said when she finished and joined him on the porch. "I made biscuits, since I couldn't find any bread. And there's pie on the sideboard."

"Thanks." Feeling awkward, he brought his hand up to curl around his left cheek. "I'll mail you your check."

"No hurry," she said as she skipped down the steps. "You can pay at the end of the week. If you make out a grocery list, I'll have my aunt pick up your supplies. Did you know you have ants in your cupboards? In the subtropics like this, it's a constant problem. I'll clean them out for you tomorrow."

This had gone on long enough. He had to tell her *now*. "Look, you've done enough. I..."

Backing away several steps, she sent him another shy smile. "Not nearly enough. The bedroom needs a good going-over. I didn't have time to scrub the shower down properly, and I can't imagine when your windows were last washed. You can scarcely see the lovely view. We'll fix all that. See you tomorrow."

Grabbing the porch railing, he got to his feet. "Really, it's not necessary."

Pausing, she scrunched up her face questioningly. "Do you like Chinese?"

Puzzled and frustrated, Blake frowned. "Chinese what?"

"Food, of course. I make a sweet-and-sour pork that melts in your mouth. Tomorrow, then." With a wave she hurried across the lawn and out the gate.

Feeling dazed, Blake could only stare after her. For a moment he nearly called out and told her to stay away. But a sudden thought stopped him.

Not once had Jenny Starbuck appeared to notice his face or his injured leg. She'd met his eyes without that guarded look so many gave him just before dropping their gaze in embarrassment. She hadn't even seemed curious. Or cautious. Just a friendly smile and a warm handshake.

And that hadn't happened to him in a long time.

Chapter Two

The disinfectant stung her nose. Turning her head aside, Jenny sneezed twice. She adjusted her rubber gloves and climbed up onto the next rung of the step stool. One more cupboard shelf to do and she'd be finished. And glad of it.

She'd found the entry hole where the ants had come in and sealed it off with some putty she'd found in the closet. Now, scrubbing the smooth wood with the large sponge, she hoped she'd gotten them all. It was a small kitchen, yet it had four sections of hanging cupboards. The job was taking her longer than she'd planned. But, as Aunt Moira often said, a job worth doing was worth doing right.

Rinsing her sponge in the basin of water, she attacked the final section. The midday sun was streaming through the window and heating the kitchen, causing her cotton shirt to stick to her damp back.

She'd worn jeans today, knowing she'd have to be climbing stools and all. Now they felt heavy and hot.

Finishing at last, Jenny stepped down. As soon as the shelves were dry, she'd have to put back all the dishes and cups she'd removed. She made a mental note to remind the captain to add ant repellent boxes to his list of supplies. This was one job she didn't want to do twice.

Emptying the basin and rinsing the sink, she sighed. He was a strange one, Blake Hanley was. She'd arrived about eight this morning only to find him already on the back porch, his walking stick in hand. She'd scarcely greeted him before he'd gone off to the beach, struggling to hide the limp that she knew must be painful. And here it was nearly noon and he hadn't returned.

It was as if he feared being around her, though Jenny couldn't imagine why. She'd been so careful yesterday not to upset him by word or deed. Although Dr. Ambrose had warned her that he might be in a temper, she'd seen none of it so far.

As she began restocking shelves, she pictured him in her mind's eye. He was quite tall, his back as straight as a rod. He was a bit too lean, which was understandable after all he'd been through. His brown hair curled down the nape of his neck, and his eyes were a shade of gray that reminded her of stormy seas. There were strain lines around the corners of those eyes, and his skin had the pale look of a shut-in. His voice had a husky quality, perhaps from the smoke of the plane crash. Jenny couldn't help but wonder how severe were the burns beneath the bandage that he was so careful to hide from her.

Watching him leave for his walk with a look of quiet determination, she'd had to admire his perseverance. The marks of pain were etched deeply on his face, yet he hadn't given up. A decidedly brave man, as Dr. Ambrose had said.

And, if he stayed out in the sun much longer, a decidedly sunburned man, Jenny thought as she glanced out the window. She hoped he'd found a shady spot, for the summer Florida sun could be brutal, especially to those unused to its powerful rays.

Shifting, she looked up, examining her work, when suddenly the stool tilted on the uneven floor. "Oh!" Jenny cried out as the stool went down and she followed it, landing hard on her rump.

"Are you all right?" Blake asked as he hurried in through the screen door. Approaching the house, he'd heard the crash and her startled cry. Still holding his cane in one hand, he reached down with the other to help her up.

"I'm afraid my dignity's hurt more than I am," Jenny said, rising to face him.

She smelled like sunshine and wildflowers, Blake thought as she looked up at him. He was close enough to notice the light sprinkling of freckles on her small nose, which gave her a youthful look. Though her eyes registered embarrassment, her mouth formed a smile, indicating she couldn't be too badly hurt.

"Thank you," she whispered as she stared into his serious gaze, realizing it was the first time he'd allowed her to look directly at his face. His forehead was pink from the sun as was his strong, square chin. Oddly she wanted to touch him, to see if her fingers could erase the traces of pain from around his eyes. But, of course, she hadn't the right and knew he'd be shocked at her thoughts. She took a hesitant step backward. "I guess I lost my balance."

"The house is old. The floor isn't smooth." Blake suddenly realized he was still holding her arm and quickly let go, then turned aside as he came out of the trancelike state he'd somehow fallen into. "As long as you're not hurt."

She allowed him the moment, sensing that he wasn't comfortable getting too close to anyone. Turning back to the cupboards, she lifted a stack of plates onto a shelf. "You must be thirsty after being in the sun so long. There's a pitcher of iced tea in the fridge, and I've put together a cold meat salad for lunch whenever you're ready."

His back to her, Blake stopped in the archway. "You don't have to provide my meals. I'm not totally helpless." She'd unnerved him with her nearness, causing him to be harsher than he'd intended.

Ignoring his tone, Jenny began hanging cups on the hooks. "You're certainly not. I'm the one not terribly surefooted, it would seem. It's just that I love to cook and I always make too much. But if you're not hungry, it's all right."

He'd never met anyone so agreeable. Suddenly contrite, he angled his right side toward her. "Actually, I am hungry. Lunch sounds great, but I need a shower first."

Jenny sent him a dazzling smile. "Fine. I'll be finished by the time you come back."

Blake found himself smiling back at her, something he hadn't felt like doing in months. Hobbling off, he couldn't help wondering just how she'd managed to get him to do that.

"I thought you were bringing Chinese today," Blake said as he sat down at his kitchen table. "Sweet-and-sour pork, wasn't it?"

"I did bring it," she answered as she set his cold meat salad in front of him. "It's in the fridge for your dinner. All you have to do is heat it."

It had been weeks since he'd shared a meal with someone. Blake found himself nervous, his eyes darting to hers regularly. Yet she still treated him as if she barely noticed his bandage, much less his limp. "I had no idea when I hired you that you'd also be cooking. The stew was wonderful. The beef had a very unusual flavor."

Jenny laughed, her eyes shining. "That's probably because it was lamb."

There was that laugh again, filling the small kitchen with music. "Lamb? No kidding. Where did you learn to cook?"

Sitting opposite him, Jenny sipped her iced tea. She hadn't planned to eat with him. But when he returned from his shower, his hair damp and smelling of soap yet with that distinctly male scent, she'd accepted his invitation to join him.

"When I was quite young, Mama's health was poor and she couldn't do much. But she'd sit at the kitchen table and tell me what ingredients to prepare and how to put together her favorite Irish dishes. Then, later, my aunt taught me more."

He saw the sadness steal over her features and remembered snatches of what Dr. Ambrose had told him. "Your mother died when you were very young, I understand."

"Yes, when I was eight. She was a wonderful woman, so patient and loving." Jenny looked up from toying with her food. "Are you close to your mother?"

He had been, once. But since his accident, he'd felt awkward being with Delores Hanley, seeing the despair in her eyes as she looked at her only child. She'd wanted to dance at his wedding, to hold his babies. She'd wailed over those lost dreams one night at his bedside, thinking him asleep. Blake swallowed a familiar lump of regret. "My mother is a good person, but she doesn't adjust well to changes." Or to disappointments. He busied himself buttering a biscuit left over from the night before.

Jenny nodded with understanding. "Adjusting to change is one of the hardest things any of us has to do. But it's the key to survival, isn't it?"

Blake looked up then, wondering how she'd learned that difficult lesson. "You mean like adjusting to the death of a parent?"

She gave a brief nod and concentrated on her food. He found himself studying her as she ate, aware that for the first time in months he was focused on someone besides himself.

Jenny Starbuck was a lovely woman, seemingly bright and quick, yet she appeared to be content doing the menial chores of a housekeeper, living in a small town that afforded few opportunities. He wondered at that contentment, which eluded him and slowed the progress of his adjustment.

"You seem to have an optimistic nature, Jenny. How do you manage that? I have trouble keeping my spirits up, as I'm sure you've noticed."

She shrugged. "I don't think it's something you consciously plan. My aunt says you're either born a brooder or not. I don't think you're a brooder by nature, Captain.''

He hadn't been until recently. But he didn't want to talk about himself. ''How did you come to live with your aunt? Did your father die, as well?'' Blake watched her eyes rise to his, saw a quick flash of pain in their blue depths before she looked away. ''Forgive me if I'm prying.''

Jenny set down her fork, finding her appetite had fled. ''It's all right. My father's still alive. After my mother died, he married again. My stepmother didn't like me, so Father bought a house for Aunt Moira and me to live in here in Apaloosa.''

Why was it that every time she thought of that period in her life, her stomach rolled queasily? Jenny wondered. It had all happened so long ago that she should have adjusted by now, she who had just informed the captain that adjusting was the key to surviving. Quickly she stood and took her plate to the sink. She wouldn't think about it, she decided.

Turning, she forced a smile. ''Do you like scones? I could make some. They're wonderful with tea.''

Obviously the subject of her background was painful. Blake knew what it was like being forced to discuss uncomfortable subjects. Banking his curiosity, he leaned back. ''Do the Irish have afternoon tea like the British?''

''Many of them do, yes.''

''Then why don't you make your scones and we'll have them with tea.'' He got to his feet, carrying his plate to the counter. ''Four o'clock, isn't that when everyone stops for tea?''

''I suppose.''

"I think I overdid the walking this morning. I'm going to rest in the lounge chair out back."

Feeling shy, yet wanting to say something, she touched his arm as he passed behind her toward the door. "Captain?"

He looked down at her, watching the sun stream in and streak her hair with gold. "Do you think you could call me Blake?"

She felt the heat of the blush rise to her face, but was helpless to stop it. She withdrew her hand, hoping he hadn't thought her too bold or possibly flirtatious. "Blake, then. I want to thank you for not pressing about my family. It's not that I'm wanting to be secretive, but some things are difficult to talk about."

She had a way of phrasing her words, an old-fashioned way undoubtedly picked up from her Irish relatives, that brought an involuntary smile to his face as he nodded. "No one knows that better than I, Jenny." Holding himself erect, he walked outside.

Through the screen Jenny watched him make his way toward the padded lounge chair in the shade of an old orange tree. Somewhat clumsily he settled himself into it, and she knew he was hurting. Such a beautiful man, she thought. Compassionate and brave. Fervently she wished she could ease his pain, but she knew only time could do that.

But she could distract him. Moving to the closet, she picked up her cleaning things. First, she'd attack his room, air out the bedding and change the sheets. Then she'd make the scones so they'd be warm and fragrant when he awoke.

Humming around a soft smile, she went to work.

Just before four Jenny made a pot of tea and set the warm scones on a plate. She'd brought a pretty embroidered cloth from home and, standing back, she decided the table looked most inviting. She went out back to get Blake.

He was asleep, looking uncomfortable all scrunched down on his weak side. Even at rest his face was creased with worry lines that gave his handsome profile a stern look. Gently she tapped his arm.

Startled, Blake sat up quickly, then grabbed at his knee as his eyes flew open. Seeing Jenny standing so close, he frowned in annoyance. How long had she been hovering there staring at him? He hated being caught unaware. "What is it?" he asked.

"It's four o'clock. The scones are ready and I've made tea." Her words were hesitant, uncertain.

"You go ahead." Deliberately he turned away from her.

She shouldn't have woken him, Jenny realized. "All right then," she said softly. Hurrying to the house, she gathered her things and left through the gate. Of course, he needed his rest. Perhaps tomorrow he'd be feeling better, she decided as she set out for home.

Hearing the gate click after her, Blake moaned aloud as he eased onto his back. Slowly he straightened his leg and felt the pain wash over him. He was hot and sticky with sweat, and his leg tingled from being too long in a cramped position. It had taken him a long while to fall asleep, and when he had, he'd slept deeply, scarcely moving.

Opening his eyes, he gazed at the gate. He'd hurt Jenny's feelings, he knew, but it would be some minutes before he could walk without aid. He couldn't have explained that without inviting her pity, and he couldn't let her see him like that. So, instead, he'd turned from her.

Having her work here was a mistake, Blake thought as he leaned forward to massage his sore muscles. Perhaps he wouldn't feel so self-conscious in front of a grandmotherly type. But what man wanted a lovely young woman to see him struggle to move around? Before, he'd have jumped right up at her first touch, grabbed her hand and hurried to the kitchen to share the tea and scones she'd made. But that was then and this was now.

Grimacing, he eased his legs over and onto the grass. Catching his breath for a moment, he picked up his cane. It simply wasn't working out. He had too much trouble relaxing when Jenny was around, and he needed to relax so he could heal. She was a distraction, one that wasn't improving his moods.

How could Chet Ambrose have thought he could simply ignore a beautiful woman—vibrant and blooming with health—marching about in his line of vision constantly? He'd been hurt, but he was still a man, a man who couldn't help reacting to the nearness of a woman. It wasn't because it was Jenny Starbuck, but simply because she was an attractive female, he told himself.

Carefully he stood and tested his footing. Using the cane, he started for the house. A woman made a man aware he should shave, that his hair needed trimming, that his shirt wasn't ironed. He didn't need all that. He was here to rest and recuperate, not impress a woman. He would tell her tomorrow.

Decision made, Blake felt better. He would thank Jenny for all she'd done, then explain that he could manage on his own from now on. Stepping onto the porch, he opened the screen door and went into the kitchen. Yes, he would...

The table was set for two, tea still warm in the pot, scones on a pale blue plate and the table spread with a snowy white cloth.

How could he hurt her again after she'd gone to so much trouble? Damn!

The second bedroom of the cottage had been turned into a study by some long-forgotten tenant. Bookshelves lined one wall, there was a large desk under the louvered window, and a comfortable leather chair with matching footstool sat beside a reading lamp sporting a Tiffany-style shade. Blake sat stretched out there on the third morning after his first meeting with Jenny Starbuck. Checking his watch, he frowned.

Always before she'd arrived by eight or quarter past without fail. Here it was nearly nine and he hadn't heard her steps on the porch, though he'd left the door unlocked.

She'd walked off hurt yesterday afternoon, and he knew he should apologize. But instead he planned just to let her know her services were no longer required and pay her off. He'd carefully rehearsed his speech to her, planning to make it brief and businesslike.

A clean break was better—for both of them. Chet Ambrose would be checking on him soon and would give him that knowing look if he discovered that Blake had hired Jenny on a daily basis. Besides, her dismissal would be better for her in the long run.

Blake was wise enough to know that. If she were exposed to the scarred and puckered flesh under his bandage, if she saw the evidence of the many surgeries that bisected his restructured leg, she would kindly but surely want to walk away on her own. Kind was what she was, just as Chet had told him. But he mustn't mistake that kindness for anything else.

For reasons she hadn't shared with him, he could see that she was lonely, too. Lonely and desperate for company or she wouldn't be so eager to share his. There had to be a story there in her past somewhere, and he wondered what it was. A woman as lovely as Jenny could have any number of men. Of course, they'd hardly exchanged stories of their lives on such short acquaintance, except yesterday briefly at lunch.

Rising, he walked to the kitchen for another cup of coffee. Where on earth was she? Filling his cup, he wondered why she didn't drive over. You could love walking and still drive to work. What if someone had stopped her along the way? Jenny had an air of innocence about her that made it difficult to believe she was twenty-five. What if a stranger...

He heard the yard gate shut, recognized her lilting voice. Quickly he made his way back to the den, not wanting her to think he'd been anxiously awaiting her. He'd told her he'd leave the back door unlocked for her. She'd undoubtedly come in and say good-morning, even though they'd parted badly yesterday, and then he'd tell her. Odd how now that she was in the house he felt less confident about sending her packing.

Back in his chair, he heard her moving around the kitchen... and he heard something else. It appeared she wasn't singing as he'd thought, but talking to someone.

Blake leaned forward, listening. Yes, by God, she was telling someone not to make too much noise in case he was asleep. Scowling, he got up. Why had she brought someone here? By now she certainly knew he wasn't comfortable with strangers. There it was—a perfect reason to fire her. Angrily he hobbled through the living room. Just when he'd been thinking that Jenny Starbuck was at least sensitive enough to read him correctly, she has to drag some stranger into his home and...

A small gray ball of fur came hurtling through the archway and all but climbed up his pant legs. Trying to protect his injured leg, Blake leaned down and picked up the squirming animal, only to have the puppy crawl up and proceed to lick his neck. "What on earth!"

"Oh, Blake, I'm so sorry." Jenny tried to retrieve her dog, but the pup was having a feast on Blake's throat. "Rafferty, what's gotten into you? I asked you to behave."

Blake's anger dissipated almost immediately, and his brows rose in amusement. "He seems to like my after-shave."

"He's not usually like this. Actually, he doesn't take to too many people. He was the runt of the litter at the local vet's where I work part-time. No one wanted him, so Dr. Swain said I could take him home. See, he has no tail." She patted Rafferty's wiggling back end. "I named him Rafferty because it means rich and prosperous in Gaelic, so Aunt Moira says. I thought he deserved a grand name, being so small."

Relieved that she'd brought an animal and not a person, Blake petted the dog's furry head while struggling over how to tell her what he'd planned to say.

"He's only a puppy," Jenny went on, as if further explanation were in order. "He hates to be locked up all day while I come here and, well, it's such a lovely day out, I just couldn't leave him. I'll keep him out of your way, really. And he's housebroken, so you needn't worry." She was babbling, she knew, and she wished Blake would stop looking at her in that odd way.

"It's all right, Jenny. I like dogs."

"You do?" She gave in to a smile of relief. "Oh, I'm so glad. I didn't want you to be angry with me."

Angry with her. He wondered if she knew how almost impossible he was finding that to be.

"About yesterday," Jenny began. "I'm sorry I woke you. It was thoughtless of me."

He had been rude to her and *she* was apologizing. Blake felt like a heel. "I...I didn't feel well," he lied.

Her brow puckered with concern. "Is there anything I can do?"

Holding the pup, Blake just stared at her. She was wearing a yellow top today with white shorts, her long, slender legs tan and smooth. Her hair was caught back at her nape with a length of yellow yarn, and her skin radiated youth and vigor. Her fresh good looks unnerved him, making all other thoughts flee from his mind.

He placed the dog in her arms. "I'm fine now. I'll be in the den reading." He turned to leave. "By the way, your scones are good."

Cuddling Rafferty, Jenny stared after him with a puzzled frown. Not exactly lavish praise, but she'd take it. He'd been smiling, seemingly pleased with the small pup, telling her he liked dogs. Then, suddenly, his face had paled and his expression had closed down—as if someone had shut off a light, leaving the room in dim shadows. Hiding secrets.

Moving to the kitchen, Jenny set the dog down. She was certain Blake Hanley had secrets aplenty and feelings he was used to hiding. She'd been hired to clean and cook for him, not to spend her time wondering. Yet she couldn't help herself. She was oddly drawn to Blake, though it was clear that he didn't feel the same.

And why should he? she asked herself as she gave Rafferty a bowl of water. A man like him, a decorated hero, should have a beautiful, educated woman of the world. She was none of those things and never would be. Heaving a sigh, Jenny shook off her mood.

She had work to do. It was a fine day to wash windows, sunny and bright. She'd seen a ladder in the back shed. Determined to stop brooding over things that were out of her reach, she went to get the bucket.

"Well, Jenny, I see the captain decided he needed your help, after all." Dr. Chet Ambrose stood with his hands on his hips, looking up at the young woman on the ladder as she finished cleaning the outside of the living room window.

"It would seem so, Doctor." At least for the time being, Jenny thought as she climbed down and placed the squeegee mop in the bucket. "There's surely enough here to keep me busy. This place has been sorely neglected."

"It's a good thing you're strong and energetic." Falling into step beside her, he strolled toward the back door. "Have you been filling him full of good food, as well?"

She smiled shyly. "He's partial to my scones."

"And who wouldn't be?" Following her into the kitchen, he glanced over at Rafferty snoozing in a patch of sunlight. "Pup's made himself at home I see." He spotted a covered dish on the counter. "Have you any scones left?"

"It just so happens I do." At the sink she washed her hands. "I'll bring some in with fresh coffee in a minute. Blake's in the den."

Chet raised a curious eyebrow. "Blake, is it?"

Jenny sent him an uncertain glance. "He...he asked me to call him by his given name."

"I see," he said in the manner of a man who sees more than the obvious. Turning, he walked toward the den.

Feeling her face heat, Jenny touched her cheeks with wet hands. Did Dr. Ambrose regret recommending her?

At the doorway to the den Chet paused, noticing that his patient was stretched out in his lounge chair, asleep with a book on his lap. Clearing his throat noisily, he saw Blake open his eyes and ease himself upright. "I hate to interrupt your sleep."

Blake made a dismissive gesture. "I sleep too damn much." In the daytime, anyway. The nights were another story.

Chet pulled up a stool and sat down. "Maybe you're taking the medicine too often."

"Nah, I hardly ever take it. I have trouble sleeping at night. Then I can't stay awake in the daytime."

"Not unusual for a patient just out of the hospital to get his days and nights confused." The doctor took hold of Blake's wrist, taking his pulse, his eyes on his watch.

"I've been out of the hospital for weeks."

"Even so." Chet stood and leaned over, his hand going to Blake's face to remove the bandage.

"Wait. Close the door."

Chet stared at him for a long moment, then closed the den door and returned to examine Blake's cheek. "It's coming along nicely. The debriding worked— there seems no sign of infection. And the last skin graft took well." From his bag he removed a handful of wrapped bandages and handed them to Blake. "Here's a fresh supply of medicated pads. Keep applying the salve the rest of the week, then stop. I want you to start leaving the bandage off for several hours each day."

Blake's eyes widened in surprise, then he shook his head. "No."

Ambrose released a ragged sigh. "A burn needs air to heal, to dry the wounds. Keeping it constantly moist with antibiotic ointment was necessary at first, but it's time for the next step. You know all this from the other transplants, I'm sure."

"I'll do it at night then."

Expertly Chet rebandaged Blake's cheek. "A little sun wouldn't hurt."

"It would sting like hell. Sometimes the heat of the sun even bothers me through the bandage."

Thoughtfully Chet zipped his bag closed and leaned forward, elbows on his knees. "How's Jenny Starbuck working out?"

Blake wasn't in the mood to go into his feelings about Jenny with his doctor. "Fine."

"I understand you like her scones."

"They're all right."

As Chet narrowed his eyes, studying his patient, there were two brisk knocks on the door. He watched Blake sit up taller and straighten his shirt as he called out to tell her to enter.

Jenny's gaze moved from one to the other. "I'm interrupting?"

"No, not at all," Chet said as he stood aside to let her in with the tray she carried. "That smells wonderful."

Blake lost the battle to avoid looking at her. She'd removed the yarn and let her hair hang free to frame her small face and trail down her back. Her cheeks were flushed from working in the sun, and she'd removed her shoes, leaving her feet bare. He swallowed hard.

Jenny set down the tray on a side table and poured their coffee, her movements graceful. She served the doctor first, then handed Blake his cup, her eyes darting to his for a brief instant. Placing the plate of scones between them, she straightened as if to leave.

"Won't you have some with us, Jenny?" Chet invited.

"Thank you, but I'm not fond of coffee." She left them alone.

"She's a hard worker, isn't she?" Chet asked between bites of his scone.

Sipping the coffee, Blake struggled with his rising curiosity, then gave in, keeping his voice low. "What do you know of her family?"

Chet wiped his hands on a napkin. "Quite a bit. Her father's Lucius Starbuck, one of the partners in a very successful Florida engineering firm. Years ago Lucius went to Ireland as part of a team hired as consultants on a bridge project. He met Annie Ryan, the daughter of one of the Irish engineers, and they fell in love. They were married and Jenny was born over there. After the project was finished, Lucius brought his family back to the states to Fort Lauderdale where he had a house. Annie's health was poor after she gave birth, so her sister Moira came along to help out. Moira was several years older and unmarried.''

"Then Annie died.''

"Yes. I hear Lucius took it real hard. But he was a man on the rise in an expanding company and he needed a wife. He married a divorcée who liked expensive things, but didn't like children. As I heard it, Moira asked Lucius if she could take Jenny and raise her on her own since the child's very presence upset Jocelyn Starbuck. Lucius wanted peace, so he bought Jenny and Moira a small house about a mile from here, and they've been there ever since.''

Blake set down his cup. "Jenny's father let her go, just like that?'' At Chet's nod he felt his mouth tighten. How could a man do that to his daughter? "And Moira never married?''

"No. She's a nice woman, decent-looking and intelligent. I believe she graduated from Trinity College. But there aren't a lot of eligible men in Apaloosa, and Moira's shy.'' He finished his coffee.

"A college degree and she cleans houses?''

"She likes to keep busy and she also works at our local library.'' Chet paused, obviously curious at Blake's sudden interest in his cleaning woman. "Did you ask Jenny about her background?''

"She told me that it was difficult to talk about some things. I can relate to that.''

Chet stood, checking his watch. "I'm sure she feels a sense of abandonment.''

Blake understood that, too, although he'd been the one to abandon his smothering family. "Thanks for telling me.''

"I've got to go." Chet's hand flew to his pocket. "I almost forgot. There was this letter for you in the mailbox at the road. I guess you don't often check for mail."

"There aren't too many people I want to hear from."

"This one's from your mother."

Blake took the envelope and studied the small, neat handwriting. He'd told his mother it wasn't necessary for her to write, that he would contact her when he felt better. She still didn't understand.

"I'll be back to check on you soon," Chet said from the doorway. "Remember what I said. Let your face get some air."

"Right. So long."

Blake sat quietly, vaguely aware of Chet saying goodbye to Jenny somewhere outside. He stared at the letter, wondering if he was up to reading it. Maybe he should just toss it aside until he felt stronger, better able to cope with the memories his mother's words would surely resurrect. Then again, what if something was wrong, someone ill?

Blake tore open the envelope.

Jenny had just finished outside and come into the kitchen when she heard a door slam very hard. Startled, she went into the living room and saw that the door to the den was ajar and Blake's bedroom door was shut. Surely he was all right in there. Perhaps he'd just touched the knob with a bit more force than necessary. She could knock, check on him. But she hadn't the right, really. This was his home, after all. She started back to the kitchen.

She was in the archway when she heard the crash. Something heavy breaking. Stunned, she twirled around, staring at his door. Rafferty came scurrying to check things out, but she caught him and scooted him outside. Returning to the living room, she hesitated near his door, wondering what to do as she strained to listen.

She heard the sound of pacing and mutterings. She could tell he was limping heavily as he walked back and forth, cursing now, louder with each word. Heart pounding, Jenny moved closer. "Blake? Are you all right?"

A loud thud hit the door, causing her to wince, followed by another thud. Objects thrown against the wood, obviously in anger.

"Go away!" Blake shouted through the door.

But she couldn't. How could she leave him in such a state? But what could she do to help him?

Another crash—sounding like a lamp this time, the base shattering on the hardwood floor. Was he intent on wrecking the entire room? Dear God, how could she stop him?

Perhaps she should phone Dr. Ambrose. He'd delivered a letter from home to Blake just before leaving, he'd told Jenny. Had something in that letter put Blake in such a temper?

The muttering grew louder as thuds hit the carpeted center of the room. Books, she decided, being yanked out of their shelves, scattering to the floor. Would he toss something through the window next? Enough.

Whether she had the right or not, she couldn't allow this to continue. The man was more hurting than angry, she was certain. Taking a deep breath, Jenny pulled open the door.

Blake stood by the bookcase, books scattered all around him. Turning toward her, his face was like thunder. "What do you want?"

Jenny hesitated in the doorway, her stomach quivering. "I want to help you, Blake. What happened?"

"Happened? Nothing much happened. Another piece of my past just blew to hell, that's all. Nothing to concern your pretty little head about." With a sweeping gesture he shoved the remaining books off the shelf.

"Please, come sit down. Let me get you something to drink."

There was whiskey in the cupboard, but even that wouldn't do the trick today, Blake thought. "They don't make anything strong enough to help me."

"Then come talk to me, please."

He laughed bitterly. "Talk? What good's talking? Doesn't change anything." Wearily he rubbed a hand over the right side of his face, his stance unsteady. "Everybody I know has talked to me. Doctors, shrinks, friends. Doesn't change a damn thing. I'm a washout, finished, no future."

She dared venture a step closer. "No, you're not. You're a fine man."

"Ha! Fine man. What do you know about me?" Blake began pacing again, his steps awkward, his limp pronounced. "Nobody knows me anymore. Nobody *wants* to know me anymore. Who can blame them? Look at me! Just look at me!"

Her heart going out to him, Jenny blinked back her tears. "I *am* looking at you. You're good and decent. You're kind and sensitive and . . ."

"No! I'm none of those things. I'm a scarred wreck, weak as a kitten most of the time. I can't walk across the damn yard without breaking into a sweat or using a cane. I can't sleep at night because of the dreams. I see the flames and hear a scream, and I realize it's mine. Was there something I could have done to prevent the crash? I ask myself over and over. And I wake up soaking wet and shaking. No wonder she doesn't want me. No one wants me." He sank onto the bed, sitting down heavily, dropping his head into his hands.

She? So that was it. A woman, someone he loved perhaps, who'd turned away from him. Jenny's hands formed fists as she struggled with a wave of anger at a woman who could hurt this man that way. Her anger gave her strength, and she moved to his side, kneeling by him, touching his arm. "If she walked away from you, it's her loss."

Blake fought the sobs that threatened to break free. He wouldn't, *couldn't,* break down in front of Jenny. Swiping at his eyes, he raised his head to look at her. "You don't know what you're saying. You don't know what I look like under all these bandages and clothes covering my scars. She didn't want to be stuck with a man like that, and I don't blame her."

Her eyes were intense and steady on his. "I do. *I* blame her. She doesn't deserve you."

He blinked, thinking he was probably hallucinating. He'd worked himself up into a state and was hearing things. Lord only knew what would be next. He had to get her out of here, to be alone, to have no witnesses to his humiliation. "Go away." Clumsily he got to his feet, nearly knocking her over. "I don't want you here."

Regaining her balance, Jenny stood. "You don't mean that."

"I *do* mean that. Go. Leave me alone."

She reached out her hand. "Please, Blake, let me help you."

Narrowing his eyes, he snarled out at her. "Don't you get it? I don't want you here. Not now, not ever again. Go away!"

Jenny stood for another moment, just looking at him. Then she turned and slowly left the room.

Weaving slightly, Blake rubbed his knee, struggling with emotions that were swamping him. Finally he heard her open and close the gate, listened to her steps as she walked away.

With an agonized cry he sank onto the bed.

Chapter Three

By seven on most June mornings in Florida the sun is already spreading its warmth on sandy beaches and shimmering on frothy ocean waves. Fishermen have taken their boats out hours earlier, and tourists stroll the streets, soaking up rays. But not so in Apaloosa. At seven the seashore was deserted as Jenny walked in the damp sand, kicking disinterestedly at fragments of seaweed.

It had been three days since Blake had sent her from his house, and she wasn't over the incident yet. During each waking hour and through the sleepless nights, she tried to rationalize his behavior. But she simply didn't know enough about his past pain to evaluate his present anguish.

She could imagine, she could guess, but she couldn't *know*. And it was upsetting her to think of him, all alone in his isolated cottage, unhappy and hurting.

She longed for a way to reach him, to help him, but hadn't come up with a solution yet. She couldn't mention the episode to her aunt. Moira's private nature would have her simply tell Jenny to mind her own business and let the poor man be.

Rafferty raced ahead of her, happily chasing the sea gulls, but even his antics did little to cheer her today. She'd spent two days working at Dr. Swain's clinic, even assisting him in an emergency minor surgery. And still her mind was with Blake—worrying, wondering. She'd considered calling Dr. Ambrose and suggesting that he visit Blake to check on him again. But she couldn't think of a way to do it without arousing the doctor's suspicions. And she felt certain that Blake would resent her telling anyone of his pain.

Shaking her hair back and raising her face to the sun, she considered the possibility that she was overreacting and that by now Blake was over whatever had upset him and back to his old self. But she couldn't make herself believe it. He'd looked at her with such agony in his eyes, spoken with such despair in his voice.

She'd only known Blake Hanley a short time, it was true, but she bled for him nonetheless. She'd grown up knowing the frustration of no one understanding how she felt. She, too, had wanted to run away and hide and, with Moira's help, had done just that. But *her* scars were on the inside, not visible for all the world to see, not like Blake's.

Jenny slid her arms around her waist and hugged herself, feeling the futility of not being able to help a man she'd come to admire and to like. What would he do if she just appeared at his house, ready to clean, as if nothing had happened? Would he—

Rafferty's excited barking drew her attention away from her musings. Climbing the sandy hill toward the trees, she called his name, hoping he hadn't found some animal even smaller than himself to terrorize. When she reached the top of the incline, she stopped in her tracks.

Blake was sitting on a jutting rock, trying to control the wiggling pup that was once more licking his neck and nearly toppling him in his enthusiasm. She noticed that he wore no shirt or shoes, only white jeans and a flustered expression.

Jenny didn't move closer, but stooped to coax back her dog. "Rafferty, come here!"

At last Blake was able to extricate the pup and deposit him on the sand facing his mistress. Obstinately the dog sat down and cocked his head at Jenny.

She had no choice but to go get him. She saw Blake hurriedly shrug into his shirt as she picked up Rafferty. But not before she'd seen the scars—some old, some more recent—on his chest and shoulders. "I'm sorry he bothered you," she said softly.

"It's all right," Blake said as he buttoned his shirt.

He kept his eyes on the ground, the left side of his body turned from her. It would seem he'd meant what he'd said, Jenny thought with a sinking heart, that he wanted her to stay away. She set Rafferty down and started past Blake.

He reached out and took her hand. "I owe you an apology."

Jenny stopped. "You owe me nothing. But I *was* worried about you."

His gaze centered on his fingers curled around hers. "I acted badly and I'm sorry. I've never done that, lost control like that."

She dropped to her knees in the sand beside his feet. "Then maybe it was time you did."

Blake released a ragged sigh. "I must have scared the hell out of you."

She held on to his hand. "I think a person can stand only so much pain, physical or emotional, and then it has to come out. When my mother was near death, she talked about dying with me, told me not to be frightened. But I was, terribly. I used to go to my room and bang my head on the wall until my forehead would bleed. Aunt Moira would find me like that, and she wouldn't know what to do. Her way to handle death was a stoic acceptance. My father was devastated. He coped by leaving the house and coming home drunk night after night. I hated him for that until years later when I understood it was just his way." She met Blake's serious gray eyes. "You've just kept too much bottled up for too long."

He hadn't expected her to understand, much less forgive him. It rocked him, the simplicity of her acceptance. Before he was aware of what he was doing he reached up to touch the silk of her cheek, then trailed his fingers along her chin. "You're a special person, Jenny."

She had never been touched by a man quite that way, never seen a man's eyes turn warm and his fingers tremble slightly as he caressed her. Suddenly her heart was pounding and her face flushing. Confused, she eased into a sitting position in the sand. "No, I'm not. But I would like to be your friend."

Blake took in a deep breath as he leaned his forearms on his bent knees. He had feared meeting up with Jenny again after that awful afternoon almost as much as he'd desired it. Had he subconsciously come to this section of beach, where he'd first seen her playing with her dog, in the hopes that she'd find him? He couldn't be sure. He only knew that the sun shone brighter when she was in his line of vision. It was too much to believe that she would choose to be near him again after that day.

"You must have a lot of friends, any one of them more cheerful and less troubled than I am."

Jenny shifted sand through her fingers. "Not so many. This is a small town. I'll bet you have far more friends than I do."

Blake looked out to sea, focusing on the waves, on the gulls swooping in and rushing back. He'd had a lot of friends, once upon a time. He had pushed them away, fearing their pity. Perhaps he'd been wrong to do that.

He was getting that faraway look again, Jenny thought. Maybe discussing the past would help. Aunt Moira always said that a person couldn't make a problem go away if they didn't state it out loud and acknowledge it. "Was that letter about one of your friends?" she asked gently.

With a sigh Blake shook his head.

"Do you want to talk about it, or should I change the subject?"

Perhaps, after all that he'd put her through, he owed her a few words of explanation. "It was from my mother, telling me that the woman I'd been engaged to is now engaged to someone else."

Her face registered immediate sympathy. "I'm sorry."

Blake watched Rafferty run in circles in the sand, chasing his missing tail. "That's not what upset me. I broke our engagement shortly after my accident. What set me off was that my mother wants me to return to Michigan, to tell Eleanor that I'll have more corrective surgery and be like I was, to try to win her back.''

"And you don't want to do that?"

"Hell, no, I don't." Blake threw a stick into the air, surprising Rafferty who raced after it enthusiastically. "Do you know how many operations I've had on this leg? Seven. And the doctors want to cut again, with no guarantees as to how many more surgeries I'll need before it'll be right. Who do they think they're kidding? My leg will *never* be the way it was before, not if they operate daily from now on. I wish my mother would learn to accept that. I have."

Had he really? Jenny was doubtful, but this was no time to mention it. "Parents can be well-intentioned and still hurt you."

Blake remembered Chet telling him that Jenny's father had let his only child move away in order to please his new wife. "Yeah, they sure can. And then there's my face. I've had so many skin grafts that there's hardly an untouched spot on my thighs and back. The last one was just a week before I got here. They want me to have more, then they want me to see a dermatologist and eventually a plastic surgeon about the scars. I might as well get a permanent room at the hospital. I'll be an old man before they're finished rebuilding me."

"Is that why you came here—to get away from all that?"

"Partly. Mostly to get away from people like my mother who think if I just cooperate, we can turn the clock back and make me just like I was before, like she wants me to be."

Sitting in the warm sand, Jenny dusted off her hands and glanced up at a circling sea gull. "That's always difficult. My father has never accepted me as I am."

Blake shifted his attention to her face. He'd seen her smiling, seen her shocked when he whirled out of control, but he'd never seen her look so wistful as she did now. "Why wouldn't he? You're a lovely young woman, intelligent and sensitive. What could he possibly find to criticize in you?"

No, she wouldn't go into her situation with Blake. He might very well turn from her just when their tenuous friendship was getting off the ground. "No fair changing the subject," she said with a smile that took the sting from her words. "Let's save my father for another day. Why did you break off your engagement right after your accident?" She thought she knew, but she wanted to hear it from him.

"I saw the way Eleanor looked at me in the hospital all burned, bandaged and possibly crippled. I sent her away before she walked away herself."

"Maybe you shouldn't have."

Blake leaned an elbow back on a smooth ledge of the rock and stretched out his left leg. "You have to understand how it was with Eleanor and me. I met her at college, the University of Michigan. She was very beautiful, a cheerleader. I was the football quarterback. We came from the same kind of family, had the same interests, the same goals. Right from the start people assumed we'd marry. They called us the perfect couple. Only one of us isn't so perfect anymore."

Jenny ignored the remark as she took the retrieved stick from Rafferty and threw it again for him. "Did you love her?"

"I sure as hell thought I did. I knew she'd make a nice home, produce beautiful children, be an asset—like my mother has been to my father. I thought that was the life I wanted and Eleanor completed the package." He shook his head wearily. "All that seems like such a long time ago."

"How do you feel about her marrying someone else?"

Sitting up, Blake shrugged. "We never could have made it together after my accident. I changed and Eleanor, like my mother, doesn't adjust well. She's undoubtedly marrying an upwardly mobile, three-piece-suit type who'll give her the kind of life she's always wanted. It's the only life she knows or wants. I wish her well."

"I feel sorry for her," Jenny said.

Puzzled, he frowned at her. "Why?"

"You may be wounded, but she's blind." Standing quickly, Jenny threw the stick as far as she could. With a yelp Rafferty ran after it.

Her statement flustered him, then he decided he was putting more importance in her words than she'd intended. Somewhat awkwardly he stood and looked after the small pup who'd gotten distracted by the sea gulls and was now chasing them. "Aren't you afraid Rafferty will run too far and not come back?"

The summer breeze lifted her hair and swirled it around her face as she looked up at him. "Dr. Swain says that if I feed him and take care of him and love him, he'll always come back to me. Animals are very loyal and a lot simpler than people."

"Aren't they, though?" The blue of the sky was reflected in her eyes, and Blake found himself lost in them. She was so lovely. Too lovely for him to start conjecturing about. But she wanted to be his friend, and he could use one. "Are we friends again, Jenny?"

With very little effort Jenny looked past the man to see the little boy inside Blake and had to fight a surprising urge to touch him, she who had never been affectionate with anyone other than her mother and aunt.

The Blake Hanley who'd been abrupt with her and destructive in his pain she could deal with. But this Blake Hanley—vulnerable and in need—reached out to her and touched her much more deeply. She was unused to the emotions he stirred in her. And she never would have guessed that his gentle question and the way he spoke her name could make her feel so funny inside.

"We never stopped being friends," she told him honestly.

He'd been feeling rotten for sending her away, like a self-indulgent, spoiled adolescent. "Will you come back and work for me? I cleaned up the mess I made in the bedroom."

She smiled at that. "I'd like to, yes. I can come now, if you like."

There was absolutely no guile to the woman, a fact that continually amazed Blake. He slipped on his shoes and reached for his cane. "Now it is."

Turning, Jenny put two fingers to her lips and whistled long and loud. In seconds Rafferty came running toward them.

"Where'd you learn to whistle like that?"

She grinned as they started out. "You will find, Captain Hanley, that I am a woman of many talents."

"I already know that." Gazing up at a cloudless sky, Blake inhaled deeply. He felt better than he had in days.

"But I hired you to work inside, not outside," Blake protested as he stood in the backyard watching Jenny yank weeds from the neglected flower bed.

"I don't recall the job description being that specific." Jenny leaned on her haunches, brushing her hair back with a gloved hand. "You like to sit out here and I want it to look nice. Besides, I love working in the garden."

He shifted his weight more to his right foot and leaned on his cane. He wasn't sure exactly why, but it bothered him to sit in his lounge chair while she worked so diligently nearby. "But it's late and you've already put in a full day inside. Look, it's growing darker by the minute."

"Yes, it usually does every evening about this time." She sent him a quick smile to let him know she was teasing. "If it'll make you feel better, you can drive me home when I'm finished." She returned to her weeding.

"You can drive yourself home, then bring the car back in the morning. That way you won't have to walk."

"But I like to walk."

"I'm not letting you walk a mile along a country road after dark."

Jenny heard the stubborn note in his voice and sighed. There was no way out of this one. "I can't drive."

Blake took a step closer, not sure he'd heard correctly. "What?"

Nonchalantly she went on pulling weeds. "I just never learned."

"Don't you find that a bit limiting?"

"Not really. I moved here when I was eight and we walked everywhere. Main Street's only a mile and a half from our house, the beach just a short distance. All the shops and places I need to go to are in between. It never seemed important."

"What about when you were at college?"

He was getting too close. Jenny felt a trickle of nervous perspiration race down her spine. "I never went to college."

"Well, high school then. I don't even know where the local schools around here are. Didn't it bother you, not being able to drive like the other kids?"

"I don't like to waste too much time envying others."

"All right, I'll teach you to drive."

"Why can't you just accept that I like to walk?"

"You can't walk everywhere. We'll start tomorrow."

She should have known better than to tell him. "You've known me two weeks and already you want to change me." Abruptly Jenny pushed to her feet. "I think I'll get a glass of iced tea. Do you want one?" Stripping off her gloves, she walked toward the back door. But a sound from the direction of the woods had her turning around. "What was that?"

Still thinking about her stubborn streak, Blake glanced up. "I didn't hear anything."

"I did. Listen." Jenny cocked her head. There it was again, a soft mewing sound filled with pain. "It's coming from the woods." She moved toward the back of the lot where the side fences ended at a thicket of trees. "Some animal's hurt."

"Don't go in there," Blake said, frowning after her. "It's getting dark—it's not safe."

But Jenny was listening for the sound in front of her, not to his warning, as she walked carefully past the first row of trees.

"Jenny, come back." Blake hobbled toward the rear of the yard. She had to be the most stubborn woman he'd met yet. "It could be a wild animal." He stared into the darkening shadows where she'd already disappeared from sight. Why was she being so carelessly foolish? And why did it bother him?

Frowning in irritation, he began to follow her. But he'd scarcely gone ten feet when he heard her steps running. She emerged, holding a furry beige thing cradled in the crook of one arm, muttering as she walked.

"Look at this," Jenny said, her voice tinged with anger. "This poor cat's had his face nearly blown off. Probably some kids with BB guns. Why can't they find something better to do than tormenting animals?"

He'd never seen her angry, certainly not over a mangy fluff of fur. He almost laughed out loud as his mouth curled in amusement. "Is that all it is?"

She stopped walking, sending him an indignant look. "*All?* What do you mean *all?*"

"I mean, it's only a cat, for heaven's sake."

"It's alive, Blake. It deserves to live just as much as you and I. No one has the right to take a life, *no one.*" The cat whimpered pathetically. She marched toward the house.

Obviously he hadn't realized how deeply she felt about this. "What do you plan to do with it?"

"Help him heal."

He watched the screen door bang behind her and swore under his breath. How could she get so worked up over a stray cat? He limped after her.

Blake found her at the kitchen sink, dampening a cloth.

"Do you have any peroxide? It's mostly his poor little nose. And maybe some antibiotic cream?"

He supposed there was no way out except to go along with her Florence Nightingale urges. He got what she asked for, even a bandage. When he returned, she was gently cleansing the wound. "Here's a medicated pad, as well. It's specially treated, so it won't stick to the wound."

"Is that what you use on your face?" She kept on gently dabbing.

"Yeah. I'm amazed he's holding so still for you."

"He senses I'm trying to help him. Animals are great that way. I once watched Dr. Swain pour antiseptic onto an open wound in this huge Doberman's side, and the dog scarcely flinched, although it must have really stung." She set the cat on the counter and examined the rest of him.

"Looks like only his face is injured."

"He was probably up in a tree looking down. Cats are so curious, which is why they're always getting hurt. The kids were probably shooting at birds." She smiled at the scruffy little animal. "There, there. Almost done."

Blake saw the animal try to back away; evidently it had had enough. "Here, let me hold him while you finish." He picked up the cat and laid him along one arm while she dabbed disinfectant on a cotton ball. The animal struggled to be free, even hissed at him, but Blake held the small head steady.

He listened to Jenny's soft murmurings as she bent to apply healing cream to the nose area. She watched what she was doing while he watched her. Her hair fell forward, curtaining her face, but he could see her forehead wrinkled with concern. "I'm surprised you didn't become a vet. You have the touch." When she didn't answer, he tried another avenue. "Have you ever thought of going into medicine?"

"No." She ripped open the medicated pad and picked up the scissors to trim it down to size.

"Why not? You'd probably be a great nurse, or a doctor."

"I'm not terribly ambitious, I guess." She shifted her attention to the cat, placing the bandage over his wound, then securing it with strips of adhesive tape.

Her aunt had a college degree yet worked in a library and cleaned houses. Was she planning to follow in the woman's footsteps? "Do you want to spend the rest of your life cleaning houses?" It seemed like a rude question, and he didn't mean to offend her, but he couldn't help wondering why she was content doing housework when she seemed qualified for so much more.

Releasing an exasperated sigh, Jenny straightened and met his eyes. "Are you unhappy with the work I've been doing for you?"

"No, of course not. But that's not the point."

"The point is, it isn't *what* we do that matters, it's how well we do it. Isn't that right, Captain?"

Blake had noticed that when she called him "Captain" she was either teasing or annoyed. She was definitely not teasing now. "I suppose so."

Looking disappointed in him, she picked up the cat and cradled him close. "Okay, Mr. No-nose. Looks like you're patched together again."

"Think he'll be able to breathe all right with only half a nose?"

"I think so. Dr. Swain treated a cat who'd been shot in the mouth recently. That rascal healed, and you should see how well he manages to eat with only a section of lip and no teeth."

"Pretty amazing."

Jenny glanced around the kitchen. "Listen, could I make a bed for him in a corner somewhere? I'd take him home with me, but Rafferty would never let him be."

Blake had never been terribly fond of cats. His father had owned beagles and hunting dogs, but never cats. Still, he didn't want to bring that disappointed look back to Jenny's face. "How about in that plastic basket in the laundry room?" he suggested.

"That'll be fine. I'll line it with clean rags."

"Do you think he's hungry? We could give him some milk." Listening to his own words, Blake frowned. How had she snared him into playing nursemaid to a cat with no nose?

"I think he needs rest more than food. By morning he'll probably be starved. Here, hold him while I fix his bed." Gently she passed the cat to Blake.

Still wary but growing drowsy, the animal didn't hiss at him this time. "Looks like you and I are twins, buddy," he told the cat. "Matching bandages and all."

Jenny heard his words and looked up, expecting to see a bitter expression on his face. But instead she saw an almost tender look in his eyes as he handed the cat back to her. After settling him in, she walked to the screen door. "I guess it's too dark to do any more yard work tonight."

Blake reached for his keys on the kitchen table. "I'll drive you home."

After one last glance into the basket, Jenny went outside.

Evening shadows danced along the pavement as Blake turned out of the drive and snapped on his lights to cut through the approaching darkness. And she had planned to walk home alone.

"I'll come get you in the morning."

It wasn't a question, but a statement. Jenny felt her back stiffen, never comfortable accepting favors. Or having decisions made for her. "That won't be necessary. The sun will be up long before I am."

"I'd still feel better. Screwballs can be out at any hour."

Now he was getting ridiculous. She tried to speak in a reasonable tone. "Blake, I haven't asked you to do anything you don't want to do, have I?" She stared at his profile, and finally he shook his head. "Then please give me the same courtesy." She glanced out the front windshield. "It's that yellow house on the left."

He eased into the drive, shifted into park and turned to her. "I just don't want any harm to come to you. Good help is hard to find."

Surprised, Jenny looked at him, saw the smile tugging at his lips and relaxed. "I'll be careful." Then suddenly his eyes darkened as he continued to hold her gaze. Again she got that shivery feeling just as she had the day he'd caressed her face. On an impulse she leaned close and gave in to the need to touch him, pressing her cheek against his. "Thank you for helping me with the cat." Fumbling with the door handle, she quickly got out, hurried onto the porch and went inside.

Left alone in the car, Blake closed his eyes for a moment, still able to smell her special scent, still able to feel her face brushing his. Why, he wondered, was he putting himself through this torture by having her around so much? The answer, when it came to him, didn't please him.

Because, difficult as it was, it was worlds better than *not* having her around.

Jenny finished the last item and turned the iron off. She reached for a hanger and carefully hung the shirt on it. Blake had told her it wasn't necessary for her to iron his clothes, but she disliked the wrinkled look. To beat the heat nearly everyone in Florida wore mostly cotton, and cotton wrinkled badly. After glancing at the dozen or so articles of clothing she'd hung on the kitchen towel bar, she folded the ironing board and put it away in the utility closet.

Actually, she rather enjoyed ironing. At home she often put a record on while she worked, usually one of her aunt's operas. The familiar music would wash over her and the time would fly by.

Moira loved opera. As a young woman living in Ireland, she had been fortunate enough to visit London and attend several live performances. Later she'd bought records and taught Jenny to share her passion, reading the libretto to the small child while they listened to the moving music together. Those shared moments were some of Jenny's best memories. Though she was fond of many, her favorite remained *Madama Butterfly*. Puccini's rich Italian lyrics never failed to stir her. She'd listened to it so often that she could sing several of the arias in passable Italian, along with the performers, though she never did so unless she was alone.

But this afternoon in the small cottage she played no music, not even the radio, because Blake was asleep on the living room couch and she didn't want to disturb him.

Putting the iron aside to cool, she glanced at the clock and realized he'd been stretched out for over an hour. After lunch she'd gone out back to water the flower beds she'd finished weeding yesterday. She was pleased that the thinned-out plants were looking better. When she came in, she'd discovered him there. She hadn't been able to resist stopping to study him a moment when he wasn't aware she was staring.

He'd confided that he often slept poorly at night, which was why he needed an occasional nap. He'd been flat on his back, one arm raised above his head almost defensively. His brow had been wrinkled as if his mind, even in sleep, were wrestling with a problem. He had shaved and nicked his chin. The small cut added a touch of vulnerability to an otherwise hard face.

Again she had struggled with a strong desire to touch him, to stroke his skin. As she had stood looking down at him, Jenny's thoughts had wandered into unfamiliar and dangerous territory. She had pictured herself sitting down beside Blake, his eyes opening and taking on that dark look of awareness. Then his slow smile, his arms coming around to hold her close. So real had been her imaginings that when she finally turned to leave the room, she'd been trembling.

What was happening to her? Jenny wondered. Never had she had such thoughts about a man. She'd brushed shoulders with doctors at the nursing home, men at the library, shopping. But she'd never been attracted enough to encourage any of them. Until now.

Vigorously she'd attacked the ironing, needing something to concentrate on rather than her mind's disturbing meanderings. The irony was that just when she found a man who could arouse her curiosity and awaken some special feelings deep within her, she was all wrong for him.

Removing the hanging clothes, Jenny walked toward his bedroom. As she passed Blake lying on the couch, she noticed that he was shifting restlessly. After depositing the clothes in his closet, she returned to find him muttering something unintelligible, his face beaded with perspiration.

Rolling onto his side, Blake reached out as if to ward off a blow. His voice was raw, ragged, his breathing labored. "Fire! We're on fire." He swatted at unseen ghosts as his head thrashed on the pillow. "Eject, Tom. Now!"

He was reliving the crash, Jenny realized. Acting on instinct, she eased onto the edge of the couch and took hold of his hands. "It's all right, Blake. It's a dream. Wake up."

But he pulled out of her grasp and his eyes popped open, wide with horror. "Goin' down. Can't stop it. Oh, God." He looked dazed, confused, then his hands flew up to cover his face.

Sharing his pain, Jenny leaned down and gathered him to her. His sobs were deep, filled with anguish, and she felt her eyes fill as she held him—just held him tightly. Rocking him gently, as she would a child, she murmured soft words into his ear, her cheek against his. "Let it out, Blake. Let it all out."

Later she couldn't have said how long she had held him like that. At last the sobs stopped and he quieted. She loosened her grip on him, yet kept his head against her chest to let him know he wasn't alone. Finally his hands lowered to rest on her arms and his eyes opened.

He'd had the dream again, Blake knew, and as he became aware of his cheek nestled into a soft female breast, he thought he must surely be having another. He felt the strong, steady beat of a heart just under his ear. Breathing in deeply, he recognized the special scent that belonged to Jenny.

Roses. She smelled of roses, the delicate aroma he recalled from his mother's garden. The fragrance wrapped around him, enchanting him. His hands moved of their own accord along her slender arms, her skin like silk beneath his fingers. How had this happened?

He'd fallen asleep on the couch and, as it so often did, the dream had sucked him in with its powerful pull. He remembered fighting the familiar demons, remembered reliving the crash that always ended in black oblivion filled with a fiery pain. But he'd never before awakened to such a wonder as this. Easing back from her, he looked into eyes as blue as the morning sky and filled with understanding.

"I used to have nightmares, too," Jenny whispered. Forgetting herself and wanting only to comfort, she raised her hand to touch his face. "I'd be damp and shaky, and my heart would be beating so loudly I thought that surely Aunt Moira in the next room must hear it.'' Her fingers trailed down his cheek and cupped his chin.

"I'm sorry if I frightened you."

Her eyes softened as she shook her head. "You didn't." Her other hand rested on his chest, and she could feel his heartbeat escalate as their shared gaze held.

She was so lovely and she was so near. Blake experienced a rush of feeling, a surge of desire that he hadn't felt in a very long time. His hands slipped around her slim waist, drawing her closer. She was near enough for him to feel her sweet breath on his cheek. In her eyes he saw a curiosity, an undisguised eagerness. Her mouth was inches from his. His throat constricted with the need to kiss her, to taste her, to lose himself in her softness.

But a shadowy memory raced across his line of vision, blocking out all other thoughts. He hadn't the right to kiss her. He was a strong, attractive man no longer. If she kissed him back, it would be out of pity—that was her way, offering comfort to any creature who needed it. Just as she had consoled the cat she'd rescued, she would kiss away his nightmare.

But he didn't want a kiss born of pity.

Averting his head, Blake drew back. Almost roughly he moved her aside. "I need to get up," he said, his voice cool.

She shifted in order to allow him to stand. He kept his eyes downcast, not wanting to see the sympathy he was certain he'd find in her gaze. With as much dignity as he could muster he walked to the bathroom and closed the door behind him.

Jenny sagged back onto the couch. She closed her eyes, feeling the old frustrations return. She should have known better than to think a man as brave, as good as Blake would want her. Her stepmother's words, spoken nearly fifteen years ago, came roaring back as if she were seated beside her.

"You're a poor, pitiful creature, Jenny Starbuck. And you'll always be a burden to someone."

Blake couldn't know, yet he'd somehow sensed that there was something missing in her. He was kind enough not to lead her on. Yet, oh, how it hurt. How badly she'd wanted to know his kiss. Just once, just this once.

Shaking, Jenny got to her feet. It was time to leave, to go home to her aunt's little house where she could be among her own things and regain a sense of self-worth. Moira had taught her that she was a good and worthy person. She would have to remember that.

In the kitchen she took Blake's dinner from the refrigerator and put it in the oven to warm for later. Then, gathering up her basket, she left the house.

Tomorrow she would be all right again, Jenny thought as she walked along. She would get over this, as she had before, and return a better person. You only make yourself sick by longing for things you can't ever have, Aunt Moira had told her repeatedly. And she was right.

She'd come back to clean for Blake, and wash and iron. But she'd keep her distance as he wanted her to. Because when he was fully recovered, he would return to Michigan and his world. There was no room in that world for someone like Jenny Starbuck. She'd been a fool to let herself dream.

Yet she couldn't help wishing she were beautiful enough and smart enough and worldly enough for Blake Hanley.

Chapter Four

Blake stepped back into the early-morning shadows of the kitchen window so that he could look out without being seen. In the backyard Jenny was hanging wet sheets on the line, talking to Rafferty who was eyeing the cat peering at him from the safety of the clothes basket. He had watched Jenny patiently introduce the two of them, then give the dog several gentle warnings about not hurting the cat, after which she murmured reassurances to Mr. No-nose that Rafferty wasn't his enemy. As the two went about their getting-acquainted routine, she kept up a steady stream of chatter to them, occasionally laughing out loud at something one of them did.

To the casual eye she was the same as always—friendly, efficient, chatty. But Blake saw the subtle differences.

She'd arrived this morning on time as usual with a polite good-morning. She'd put together a pot of chicken soup that even now was filling the kitchen with appetizing smells. She'd set about gathering the laundry, answering any questions he sent her way, helpful as ever.

Only the light had gone out of her eyes.

Blake felt like hitting something hard. He never should have let things go so far yesterday on the couch. Admittedly he'd been taken aback, awakening from a nightmare to find his head resting on her soft breast. But he should have been strong enough to back away from her immediately.

He'd almost kissed her. What was wrong with him? He was hardly a teenager touching his first woman. He knew better than to allow himself to get close to someone again. Eleanor's legacy lived on. It had been a physical reaction, that was all.

Yet he'd managed to hurt Jenny again, though he wasn't sure just how. Surely his stopping when he had couldn't be the cause of her cool attitude since. Despite her earlier denials, he knew she must have men friends. So why would she want to kiss him—a battered, beaten man?

No, a friendship was all right, but more was out of the question. He was never going to open himself up for that kind of rejection again. However, for reasons he had difficulty defining even to himself, he enjoyed having Jenny around, despite the fact that she inadvertently had him yearning regularly. He'd always stood alone, not really needing anyone, not in the most profound sense. But now he found he needed a friend, just one. One who didn't judge him too harshly and showed no signs of pity.

Before, people had gravitated toward him and he hadn't had to work at keeping friends. Now he felt like a fish out of water. He wished he knew what to say to make Jenny smile at him the way she was smiling at those two animals. Standing and watching her, an idea began to slowly take shape.

Finished with the wash, Jenny went in, settled the cat in his basket and walked to the stove to check her soup. As she added seasonings, Blake joined her.

"Would the soup be all right if you turned it off for a while?" he asked as he opened the refrigerator. He took out some cheese and bread and set them on the counter.

She glanced at him curiously. "Why would you want me to do that?"

"Because we're going fishing." Quickly he rolled bread around chunks of cheese.

"Fishing?"

"Uh-huh." Blake looked over at her, then reluctantly tore his eyes away from her soft curves under the blue terry-cloth top she wore over well-washed jeans.

"What are you doing?"

"Getting our bait together." Finished, he stuffed his makeshift bait into a paper sack. "I remember spotting a couple of poles in the shed." He walked outside, pleased to see that her curiosity had her following him. "Ah, yes, here they are." He pulled out the poles and checked the lines.

"Why exactly are we going fishing?"

By now he knew the best way to get to her was by appealing to her desire to help someone. "Because I'm going to go stir-crazy if I don't get out of this house

more, and it's not as if I have a large number of activities to choose from. But I think I can handle a pole."
He looked into her puzzled eyes. "Don't you like fish?"

"Well, yes, but..."

"Good. You've been cooking for me. Now tonight I'll cook for you." He started walking toward the beach. "Wait until you taste my sautéed fish fillets. I'll even attempt to make hush doggies."

Following him, she laughed. "I think you mean hush *puppies*." Touching his arm, she stopped. "Blake, why are you doing this?"

"Because you've been working hard, and I thought it would be nice if two friends spent the day together doing something that requires very little effort."

"But what about your leg?"

"You don't need two good legs to sit on a dock and dangle a fishing line. Do you think my scarred face will scare away the fish?"

"Of course not." Hesitancy gave way to an easy grin.

"Well, then, let's go." He heard a bark of protest from behind the kitchen door and smiled to reassure Jenny. "Rafferty will be just fine. There's nothing he can hurt in there."

Relenting, she walked with him the short distance to the weathered pier that stretched out far into the water. They chose a spot near the end and sat down. Jenny raised her face to the sun while Blake attached the bait to the hooks. When he finished, he handed over her pole. She regarded it suspiciously. "I've never done this before. What do I do?"

"Just toss out the line and wait. The fish do the rest." Demonstrating, he threw out his line. It arced, then dropped into the water. In moments the bobber reappeared.

Jenny followed suit, then sat back and leaned against the post railing. They were silent for several minutes. "Sitting here like this reminds me of one of my favorite books, *The Old Man and the Sea.*"

Blake shifted to look at her. "Hemingway. One of my favorite authors. But I like some of his earlier works better, like *The Sun Also Rises.*"

She shook her head. "His main character was too lost in that one, too tortured."

"That's probably why they said he wrote about the lost generation, usually about men searching for some meaning in life." Blake stretched out his leg. "I guess that theme could apply to the present as well as the twenties."

He was getting that introspective, cloudy look again. Jenny sought to lighten the mood. "How long does it usually take to catch the first fish?" she asked.

"Sometimes ten minutes. Other times all day."

"A patient person's sport, I see."

"I'm patient, for the most part. Teachers have to be."

"I thought you were a pilot."

"At first. Then a flight instructor. I majored in education in college."

"I suppose one day you'll go back to teaching then, perhaps at a college or high school."

Blake looked suddenly reflective, as if he hadn't considered that far ahead. "I don't know. For months now I've only been focused on getting well again. I've scarcely thought beyond that."

"I'll bet you're a very good teacher."

"What makes you think so?"

Jenny slipped off her sandals and dangled her bare feet in the water. "Oh, I don't know. You have an authoritative way about you and yet you're sensitive. Too many teachers are just interested in stuffing information inside a child's head long enough for them to be tested and then moving them on, not caring whether they really understand what they're learning. And if they run across a child that's different, they just want them out of their classroom, to send the problem to someone else." She sighed. "I suppose it's because of overcrowded schools."

"You sound like you're speaking from experience."

She shrugged and abruptly shifted her gaze out across the ocean. "It's on the television news nearly every night. Children go through twelve years of schooling, pass all kinds of tests, and many can't qualify for the simplest of jobs. Teaching should be a calling, like medicine or the priesthood, I've always thought."

"I suppose you're right. It sounds like a field *you'd* enjoy."

She ignored his attempt to probe. "You see, Aunt Moira attended Trinity College in Ireland and qualified for a teacher's certificate. Yet when she came here and wanted to teach, they told her it wasn't enough, that she needed more credits and more testing. Such a shame, since she's so good with the children at the library."

He had wondered about Moira. "She didn't go back to college here just because she was annoyed at their regulations?"

"Not exactly. She had me to take care of and she didn't have much money. She refused to ask my father for more. So she went to work at the library because I could go there with her."

"I see, you mean after school. But then why did she go to work for Dr. Ambrose?"

Jenny shifted into a more comfortable position, hoping she wasn't backing herself into a corner with this conversation. "Small-town libraries don't pay very well. And Dr. Ambrose gives us both free medical care in return for housework. He's been very generous to us."

"I can't imagine your father not being aware of your needs. Doesn't he come visit?"

"He did, at first, and he'd give Moira some money. Mostly he just calls now and then. He's not a *bad* man. Just very busy. He and Jocelyn travel a lot."

Not *bad*, oh no, Blake thought. Just selfish, self-centered and neglectful. Didn't the man have a conscience? None of his business, he decided, yet he hated seeing that haunted look in Jenny's eyes. He was surprised to find himself searching for a way to divert her. Lounging back against the post, he let his gaze sweep out to sea. "Wonder what that is?" he asked lazily. "Do sharks ever come this far in?"

Jenny swung around so quickly that she nearly toppled into the water. "Where?"

Blake struggled to keep his features even as he pointed to a spot in the distance. "Out there. Could that be a fin sticking out of the water?"

Straining her eyes, she peered intently. "I don't see a thing." As she continued searching the surface, she heard a low chuckle. Turning, she saw Blake grinning. "Shame on you. You tried to scare me." It was the first spontaneous, open smile she'd ever seen from him, and it took her breath away. How handsome he was when he let himself relax a little.

Blake laughed at her indignant tone. "I almost had you there for a minute."

"Not really. I . . . oh!" Jenny sat up straighter, feeling a tug on her line. "I think I've got something."

He leaned closer to help her. "Go slowly now and reel it in. That's it. Keep the pole anchored and reel."

Excited, she kept cranking. In a few minutes her catch emerged from the frothy sea. A very soggy hightop tennis shoe. Disappointed, she stared at it. "Well, shall we bake it or fry it?"

Blake reached for the line to remove her messy catch. "The first one never counts, anyway." With a high-arced throw he sent the shoe back to its watery grave, then dug into the sack for more bait. "Let's try again."

Jenny settled back, tossing her line out again. "I'm not sure there's anything else out there, except maybe that shoe's mate."

"Patience," Blake said, sitting back. "A successful fisherman has to have patience."

By five o'clock they'd run out of both patience and bait. The clever fish had somehow managed to nibble their offerings from the hooks without getting caught. "Good thing you made that soup, after all," Blake said as he rose to his feet awkwardly, hanging on to the railing until the numbness in his left leg passed.

"Great sport," Jenny commented. "I can see why people spend hundreds of dollars on expensive fishing gear to come out here and do this during their vacation."

"Some days they aren't biting no matter what you do," he explained as they started back. Turning to look at her, he frowned. "Looks like you got a little too much sun today." Her face was pink, as were the V of her neckline and her arms. "I should have dug up a hat for you."

Jenny touched her cheeks as they walked through the gate and on into the kitchen. "It doesn't hurt."

"It probably will. I think there's something that'll soothe it in the medicine cabinet."

In the bathroom Jenny found the bottle. "This is a really dumb thing for a Florida resident to allow to happen. I *never* sunburn."

"You did today." Coming up behind her, Blake took the bottle from her and poured a small amount of the white liquid into his palm. He touched her arm to apply the medication, but she squealed and jerked back. "Does that hurt?"

"No. It's just cold."

"Try to be brave." He spread the soothing liquid onto her arms. Even over the medication's aroma he could smell her scent in the close confines of the small bathroom. She smelled like sunshine and warm woman. Blake swallowed as he tipped her chin up so he could tend to her red nose.

Gently he smoothed the cream over her forehead, cheeks and nose, then down around her chin and neck. When he touched the pulse pounding at the base of her throat, he stopped. Slowly he raised his eyes to meet hers. Dark blue and conspicuously aware, they watched him.

Feeling suddenly brave, Jenny's hand covered his and brought it down between them. Her lips trembled with tension held in check, but she had to ask, even if he said words she didn't want to hear. Surely it would be better than this terrible yearning to know. "Yesterday you almost kissed me. Why didn't you?"

She had to bring that up. He dropped his gaze and busied himself capping the bottle. "Because it wouldn't have been right."

Jenny looked honestly puzzled. "Right? I don't understand."

"A man shouldn't take advantage of a woman. You were offering me comfort, not passion." He wished he had a better explanation to give her.

Comfort? At first, perhaps, but then she'd been offering him . . . what? Not passion, exactly, for she'd never known it. Her trust, perhaps hesitantly offered so that he might show her what a kiss could be between a man and a woman, and help her understand the impatient new feelings that churned inside her. But obviously his love of teaching didn't extend to this area.

As Blake stood watching her, she studied his features in the strong light of the bathroom. The burns on his face had been limited to his left cheek, beginning just below his eye and curving slightly around his jawline. At least that was the area he kept bandaged. The rest of the skin was untouched. His right cheek showed the bristles of a day's growth of beard. His gray eyes were as dark as pewter and tinged with regret. But it was his mouth that commanded her attention, his lips full and inviting. She wondered how they would feel touching hers, whether they would be gentle or firm and insistent. She would never know; Blake didn't want her to know.

With a shaky hand Jenny put the cream away. "I'm sorry if I embarrassed you."

He stepped back and out of the bathroom. "You didn't."

She followed and, at the kitchen door, turned to face him. "At least I understand now." She left quickly, skipping down the stairs and heading for the gate.

Blake stood watching her leave him once more, gripping the doorframe. She understood nothing. *Nothing.*

"There you are, lass," Aunt Moira said as Jenny walked into the kitchen. Seated at the table, she closed the book she'd been reading. "I waited for a while, then decided you were eating supper with the captain again and went ahead without you. But there's cold chicken and salad in the fridge if you're hungry."

Food was of no interest to her at the moment. "I'm not hungry." Jenny got herself a cup and sat down opposite her aunt, pouring herself tea from the ever-steeping pot, then topping off her aunt's cup.

"You look tired, Jenny. I told you to call me and I'd come get you, save you from walking so far after a day's work."

"I didn't work much today. We went fishing this afternoon." She touched her warm cheeks with both hands. "I got a bit too much sun."

"So I see." Moira removed her reading glasses and turned her shrewd gaze to her niece. "Fishing, is it? Now, why would you be doing that?"

Jenny took a sip of tea before answering. "Blake said he was going stir-crazy sitting in that cottage day after day. But as it ended up, the fish weren't biting."

"So you came home empty-handed. Surely that isn't why you're looking so down-in-the-mouth?"

She sighed heavily. "No, it's Blake."

"Blake?" Moira sat up taller. "What's he done, lass?"

"Done? Nothing. It's just that he tries to hide it, but I know he's unhappy. It hurts me to see it." Jenny brushed back her hair, feeling herself near tears, wondering at her own emotional state. She rarely cried. "There was a woman who turned from him after he was hurt. I think he's afraid to let anyone else get close to him, to comfort him."

Moira took a deep breath and leaned back in her chair, her expression worried. "Just how had you in mind to comfort him?"

Jenny shook her head. "It's not what you're thinking. He's not laid a hand on me, nor does he wish to. He treats me like a young sister. And I want so much to help him."

"Ah, but you are, lass. You keep his house clean, wash his clothes and cook his food. That's all he'll be needing for a while, that and rest. When his body heals, his mind and heart will follow."

Jenny sipped her tea thoughtfully. "The wounds inside take longer. People are thoughtless. They've said things and hurt him. He feels unattractive and a bit lost, but he shouldn't. He's tall and straight and stronger than he thinks. His eyes can warm you quicker than the sunshine, and his laugh—the few times I've heard it—is wonderful. I wish I could convince him."

Moira's worried frown deepened as she reached over to take her niece's hand. "Child, need I remind you, you were hired as a housekeeper, not as a healer of body and soul? You should concentrate on the house, not the man."

"Oh, but I can't ignore the man, Aunt Moira. He's so kind, so special. You should see him with Rafferty. The dog leaps up on him and licks him constantly. Animals have a sixth sense, you know. They recognize the good in people. Blake doesn't even like cats, yet he puts medicine on Mr. No-nose even as the cat snarls and hisses at him. Then, when he doesn't think I can hear, he talks to him, trying to win him over."

"I understand that he's a good man, Jenny. But you're getting in over your head. You mustn't let yourself care too much for someone who's here for a brief time only, to heal his body and then go back where he belongs. He's from another world, lass. You'll only be letting yourself in for grief if you let this continue."

Jenny blinked back the moisture as she met her aunt's troubled gaze. "How do you turn off your feelings, Aunt Moira?"

Feeling a bit dazed, Moira just stared. "You've gone and done it now, haven't you, Jenny lass?"

"Done what?"

"You've fallen in love with a man who can only bring you pain, just as your mother before you."

"No, that can't be. Love is supposed to make you happy. What I feel for Blake makes me sad. And, besides, we're just friends." She drained her tea, then looked at her aunt. "What do you mean about my mother? Did my father hurt her?"

"Yes, child, he did. But that's a story for another day." Moira stood and carried her cup to the sink. "It's you we're discussing this day." As Jenny came alongside, she turned to her. "I think it might be best if you stopped working for the captain, before you get in deeper. You know I only want what's best for you."

Jenny dropped her gaze and slowly shook her head. "I can't, Aunt Moira. I can't walk away from him." Instead, she turned and walked away from the kitchen, heading for her room.

Moira sighed. "I thought not," she said aloud in the empty room. "It's already too late."

He heard the music even before he entered his backyard. Someone was playing the piano, someone quite talented. He walked through the gate, listening to the rich sounds drifting out through the open windows. It had to be Jenny, for he knew by now that she never brought anyone over except Rafferty. He'd had no idea she was so accomplished.

Making his way onto the porch, he stopped in the kitchen to have a glass of lemonade. Since their afternoon of fishing last week, he had kept his distance from Jenny, taking a book along to lengthen his walks by stopping to read in the shade.

There was no longer that much to do in his small house since she had cleaned it thoroughly when she first started. So if he stayed in his den mornings while she worked and went to the beach after lunch for a couple of hours, she was usually ready to leave when he returned. The arrangement didn't please Blake, but he hadn't been able to dismiss her. He had even stopped asking himself why.

Walking into the living room, he paused near the piano as she finished playing a haunting piece from the musical *Cats*.

Jenny glanced up, her eyes taking on that hesitant, guarded look he'd noticed of late. "I hope you don't mind if I took a break and played your piano."

Blake shook his head, noting there was no sheet music in front of her. "You're very good. Where'd you learn to play like that?"

"My mother began teaching me, then Aunt Moira took over. She loves all kinds of music—opera, show tunes, classical. She spends all her spare money on records. We have a huge collection."

He leaned forward, bracing his elbows on the piano top. "And the sheet music, too, or do you play by ear?"

Jenny's fingers trailed along the keyboard lightly. "By ear."

"I'm impressed. Play another piece."

"What would you like to hear?"

"How about something by Gershwin?"

"Porgy and Bess?" She moved into "Summertime" effortlessly, watching her hands as they moved over the keys.

He listened, entranced. She was full of surprises, and far more well-rounded than he'd first thought. As the last notes sounded, she sent him a shy smile. "That was lovely, Jenny. Thank you."

She rose. "I have to finish up in the kitchen." Sliding off the bench, she left the room.

Blake walked to the den and slumped into his chair. He wasn't hot as much as sticky, and he longed to remove his shirt. But he couldn't while Jenny was still in the house. He wouldn't invite her pity by letting her see his scars.

While only his left side had been burned, his unclad body still was a far cry from the smooth skin over hard muscle that he had once taken for granted. On his back, left arm and shoulder were a mixture of skin grafts, donor sites and the thicker keloid scars. In time, he'd been told, the hard scars would soften and the red color would fade to a more natural pink. However, at this stage he had no desire to display them to anyone.

Right now, more than anything, he wanted to remove the itchy bandage from his face. Dr. Ambrose had been right that air was the best thing for his cheek. Out in the sun moisture built up under the medicated pad, making him uncomfortable.

He looked down at the packet of pads and antibiotic cream on the table beside him. He could hear water running in the kitchen and decided Jenny was busy. He'd have time to at least change the bandage before she came to say goodbye for the day. Carefully he pulled off the gauze covering, then the damp medicated pad. He picked up the hand mirror he kept there and studied his face.

The skin was mottled, of course, and the two thick keloid scars were a dark red and still hard. Around the edges the skin grafts had taken and were nearly healed. And the...

"I brought you some lemonade," Jenny said from just inside the doorway.

Blake nearly dropped the mirror. Turning his head quickly aside, he muttered his thanks.

Jenny moved closer. "Let me do that for you."

"No! I can do it myself."

She set his drink down. "I know you can. But my hands are cleaner than yours. Shouldn't healing burns be kept sterile?"

He clamped down his annoyance. "Yes. Jenny, I can manage. Just leave me be."

But she was having none of it today. Pulling up the footstool, she sat down facing him. "Don't turn from me, Blake. There's no need. I've seen much worse. We're friends, remember?''

He let out a ragged sigh. ''There's a limit to what friendship includes.''

''Let me ask you something. If our positions were reversed here, if it were my face that was burned, would you turn away from me?''

''Of course not. But...''

''I realize I'm not as experienced as you are in many things, but I'm not a hothouse flower, either.'' She picked up the plastic container. ''Is this what you use?''

He wanted to strangle her. All right, he would give her a shock she would long remember. Slowly he turned so that he was facing her directly. He watched her intently.

Jenny met his eyes. ''Is this a solution of some sort?'' she asked, still holding the container.

''Sterile water. I put some on a piece of gauze to clean the area, then either apply antibiotic cream or spray.'' To his surprise she wasn't flinching, nor had her expression changed in the slightest. But she hadn't touched him yet, either, or felt the coarse, uneven skin.

Jenny dampened a gauze pad with the sterile water, then leaned forward. ''Let me know if this hurts.'' Gently she dabbed the area, her touch light. The pad absorbed the accumulated moisture while it cleansed the burned area. Finishing, she raised her eyes to his watchful gaze. ''Do you want cream or spray?''

''The cream.''

''Can I apply it with my fingers?''

''Yes. It's no longer an open wound.''

She unscrewed the cap and dipped two fingers into the antibiotic cream. Again she leaned forward and lightly spread the cream over the entire area, working unhurriedly. "Dr. Swain treated a terrier puppy last year whose front legs had been burned in a kerosene fire. After the wounds stopped draining, the owner was told to use the open-air method of healing. No bandages unless the dog was outside where he might get dirty and infect the area."

She wiped her hands on a tissue and recapped the jar. "I'm not a doctor, but I think you should let the air get to your face and leave the bandage off."

Blake leaned back wearily. "You don't know what you're talking about. You don't know what it's like to face people looking like . . . like some freak in a sideshow. You were curious, and now you've seen. Don't I repulse you?"

"No." She said it so simply, so calmly, he could only stare.

"Are you blind, woman?" When she didn't answer but just sat there quietly looking at him, he ran an angry hand through his hair. "Ah, what would you know about adjustments, about people turning from you in disappointment?"

Jenny rose and moved to the door, her expression suddenly sad. "More than you might think. Not all scars are visible, Blake."

For long minutes after she was gone, Blake sat staring at the spot where she had stood. What, he wondered, had she meant by that?

Chapter Five

Blake watched a wide-winged pelican swoop down from the sky, dip into a frothy wave, then rise again with breakfast in its pouch. It was a cloudy morning, a nice change from the unrelenting summer sun. And his thoughts were equally cloudy.

He had sat for a long while last night after Jenny left, thinking about her and what she'd said. Thinking about her touch and the way she had cleaned his scarred cheek. She really should pursue a career in some field of medicine. She was a natural, instinctively compassionate, kind.

That was all it was, of course. A woman with a sympathetic touch administering to a patient. Her hands were strong yet gentle, and though he longed for them to touch him as a man and not an invalid, he knew he shouldn't encourage her. He shouldn't waste his time and limited energy longing for something that would be a mistake for both of them. Hadn't his therapist at Brooks Medical Center told him that severe burn victims had to learn to accept certain losses before they could accept life again?

He was evidently a poor study, Blake decided as he stretched his left leg in the warm sand. And a poor patient, too. Chet Ambrose had phoned early that morning before leaving for hospital rounds. He was still too busy to stop in, he said. But, more to the point, he thought it was high time Blake stopped in his office, anyway—for a complete physical, so he could report back to his brother in San Antonio. As soon as possible.

Blake rubbed at his knee, feeling the raised scars through his cotton slacks. So many times under the knife, yet his surgeon wanted to cut again. Frank Ambrose had given him dire warnings that if he let things go too long, his leg would heal improperly. It would be shorter than the other, and he'd end up with a permanent limp. Blake knew all that. He also knew that going in for the exam would start both doctors urging him back to the hospital. What he didn't know was if he could face it all over again.

Fighting a shudder, he stared out to sea, remembering those blurry days right after the crash. Gradually they'd taken him off the morphine, fearing addiction, and then pain had become his constant companion. He had lived in dread over the changing of his dressings every three hours, the sound of the sobs he tried to hold back. He was always cold, always wet, the smell of burned flesh ever present in his darkened room. He'd fought off pneumonia, kidney failure and sieges of delirium while his body struggled to heal itself.

After a few weeks, they had transferred him to the Stryker frame, the stretched canvas bed invented especially for burn victims and some paralyzed patients. He was never alone then, sandwiched between two sheets, turned regularly by round-the-clock nursing. He remembered the sense of isolation brought on by the necessary precautions taken to avoid infection.

But, most of all, he recalled Major Ambrose's deep voice. "You will live, Blake. You will recover. You will walk again." Some days he would believe him; most he wouldn't. But the good doctor had been right. And now he wanted Blake back for more pain. No thank you, Doctor.

Picking up his walking stick, Blake got to his feet. Because of the cloud cover it was unusually humid; although he hadn't been out long, he was ready to go in. He would shut himself up in his study until Jenny finished, then drive her to the store so she could pick up groceries. The cupboards were getting bare.

Perhaps it would rain later, he thought as he entered his yard. His aching leg was better than a weather barometer. In the kitchen he poured himself a glass of iced tea and stood sipping it.

Glancing over, he saw the note he'd left for Jenny still on the table. He had asked her to make up a grocery list so they could shop, but he didn't see her list anywhere. He could hear her humming in the front of the house as she dusted. Maybe they should go now so he could spend the afternoon reading.

"Jenny," he called out, walking to find her. "Did you make out the list?"

Feather duster in hand, she emerged from the den. "Good morning, Blake. I don't remember talking with you about a list."

"The note I left you on the kitchen table, didn't you read it?"

She colored slightly, then her eyes skittered away from his. "No. I must not have noticed it."

"I don't see how you could have missed it." He ran a tired hand through his hair. "Make it out now, will you? I'm going to change my shirt and then we can get to the store. Looks like it might rain, and I'd like to avoid being out in it."

Five minutes later he found her in the kitchen, staring out the window. When she heard him, she swiveled around. "Why don't I just tell you what we need and you write it down? My handwriting is terrible."

Blake felt a flash of annoyance. He'd been cross ever since Chet's call earlier, and the morning wasn't improving. "Look, I don't feel like playing games today. Write out the damn list and let's go."

He was wearing the bandage again and his brows were drawn together, giving his angular face a stormy look. Jenny's hand fluttered to her throat nervously. "I . . . I don't need a list. I have a very good memory. I'll just go into the store and get what we need."

"Damn it, Jenny, why are you being so stubborn? Why can't you just make a list? You know I hate to go into town and, good memory or not, you're liable to forget something." He thrust the pad and pen at her.

Stunned, she took it, looking down at the paper as if it were foreign to her.

Clamping down on his irritation, Blake opened the refrigerator and looked inside. "We need eggs and there's no milk. The catsup's almost empty and . . ."

She hadn't moved, just stood there, her blue eyes huge and vulnerable.

"What's wrong with you, Jenny?"

With an odd sound from deep in her throat, she tossed the pad and pen down on the counter and ran around him. Before Blake was altogether aware of what had happened she was out the door and down the steps. Slamming the refrigerator closed, he hurried after her.

He never would have caught her with his injured leg if she hadn't had trouble opening the gate in her haste. As she fumbled with it, he caught her arm and swung her around. "What on earth is wrong?" he demanded, then stopped. Tears were running down her cheeks as she shook her head.

"Nothing." She took in a shaky breath. "Everything." Losing control, she felt a sob take her and averted her gaze.

Uncertain what to do with her, Blake tipped her chin up, forcing her to look at him. "Tell me what's wrong."

Jenny shook her head, tears streaming from her eyes. "I can't. Please don't ask me anymore." Breaking away from his hold, she turned to grapple with the gate latch again.

His anger rising, Blake grabbed her and whirled her around. This was plain ridiculous. "Jenny, talk to me."

"Let me go." Struggling against him, she swiveled, but his arms went around her and tightened. In her anxiety to be free she shook her head wildly, her long hair brushing across his face.

"Not until you tell me what's wrong." Shifting her in his arms, Blake pulled her against his chest, pressing her head to his shoulder. "Whatever it is, we can work it out."

He was only making things worse, Jenny thought as the sobs she couldn't prevent came bursting through. "No, we can't work it out." Her chest heaved with the effort to keep a small shred of control as her hands twisted in the fabric of his shirt. "I just want to go, please."

His face bending to the fragrance of her hair, Blake stroked her back. "I can't let you go like this." Easing away from her, he leaned down till his face was close to hers. "It's okay, Jenny. Don't cry." He moved his hands to frame her face, his thumbs brushing away her tears. "Please don't cry."

But she couldn't stop. "Oh, God," she moaned, then clutched at him and buried her face in his neck. Clinging to him, she felt the shame wash over her, felt the hideous helplessness. She couldn't tell him. She simply couldn't.

He was murmuring to her, trying to soothe her, she knew, his arms so strong around her. He was just being kind, but her body didn't know that and it was beginning to respond to his nearness, to his maleness. She'd never been held this close, not by a man who attracted her. Jenny felt her blood heat as, slowly, she drew back from him.

For the space of a heartbeat Blake studied her tear-streaked face—the raw vulnerability in her eyes—and forgot he'd been comforting her. He lowered his mouth to hers.

She stiffened, a shocked sound rising from her throat. Blake loosened his grip slightly, softening his lips and urging a response from her. Another moment and he felt her tense muscles begin to relax. The hands he'd thought might push him away now crept up his back and drew him closer. When her lips parted a fraction, he eased his tongue inside.

Creeping warmth invaded Jenny's limbs as her blood raced and her pulse pounded. So this was what it was like, she thought through a haze of feeling. This was what it was like to have your energy seep away yet feel incredibly more alive. This was what she'd been wanting to know, to experience. In a rush of feeling she moved her mouth under his and kissed him back. Head spinning, she let him take her where she'd never been.

Blake felt the change in her as his hands wandered into the silk of her hair. Since he'd first seen her, he had wanted to run his fingers through the rich strands. He nearly groaned aloud as her tongue finally touched his—shyly at first, then more boldly. His body, too long denied, surged in response.

He shifted, raining kisses over her face, down the smooth line of her throat and, with a soft moan, returned to capture her waiting mouth. Instinctively she responded, her breathing as ragged as his. His hands slid down her slender back and pressed her to him, his whole body throbbing with need.

Jenny heard warning sounds going off in her mind, the kind repeated often enough in her teens by her concerned aunt, but the sensual pull of Blake's kiss blocked out all caution, all thought. How could she have known that a man's mouth could work such magic, that his hands could make her soft and pliable with just his touch, that his hard chest rubbing against her breasts would cause such an ache?

She felt a sudden yearning that was almost unbearable, and she wanted these feelings to go on and on. Yet her fierce reaction frightened her. She wrenched herself free of his arms and stood struggling for breath.

Equally stunned, Blake stepped back. "I...I didn't mean for that to happen."

What did he mean by that? she wondered. That he was sorry he had kissed her, had held her so intimately? That had to be it. A blush of humiliation deepened her color as she turned and finally managed to open the gate. Without another word she ran through and headed for the road.

This time he let her go. Dazed, Blake stood with a hand braced on the fence. What had happened to upset her in the first place? And how had he let himself be drawn into kissing her?

Hobbling back inside without his cane, he acknowledged that he had wanted to kiss her for days now. Strictly a celibate male longing for an available woman, that was all, Blake told himself. But that didn't make it right. Jenny was sweet and appeared quite innocent. She'd responded to him hesitantly, not in an experienced way. And he'd probably frightened her, so she'd run.

Easing into a chair, Blake let out a deep breath. He was still trying to beat down his body's reaction to holding Jenny. He was also wrestling with the feelings she'd brought to the surface. He didn't want to feel anything for her. He was a mess, physically scarred from his accident, emotionally drained from encounters with his family and Eleanor. He hadn't yet worked out how he was going to cope with the new life he'd have to build around his limited capabilities.

Dealing with all that was enough. He didn't need to get interested in a woman and all that a relationship involved. It was just a kiss, he reminded himself. Not a big deal.

Then why was his heartbeat escalating at merely the memory? And why was his hand still trembling?

This was stupid. Blake stood and poured himself another glass of iced tea. He would wait a while, give her time to calm down, then go talk with her. He'd be a big brother to her, find out what was troubling her and help solve it. And he'd keep his hands off her.

An hour later, when he turned into her driveway, he found Jenny sitting in the backyard swing, her dog cuddled in her arms. Rafferty jumped down and ran to greet him as he got out of the car and walked to her. Blake bent to pet the pup, then stopped in front of Jenny. "May I sit with you?" he asked.

Jenny scooted over to the far side of the two-seater. Somehow she had known he would come. Blake Hanley was a man who kept hammering away until he found out what he needed to know. She had already decided she'd have to tell him. What she hadn't figured out was how she was going to handle herself when he turned from her, when she saw the disappointment on his face.

He sat down, then started the swing moving gently with his good leg braced on the grassy ground. He was near enough that she could smell his after-shave, and if she closed her eyes, she knew she could instantly recall his special taste. She should never have kissed him back, never have allowed herself to know what it felt like to be held by him. Watching him walk away would be infinitely more difficult after being in his arms.

Jenny knew he was waiting for her explanation. She cleared her throat and kept her eyes on the grapefruit tree alongside the drive. "I acted badly," she began. "I'm sorry I left like that."

"I'm the one who should be apologizing. It wasn't right, my kissing you like that."

Why? Why was it wrong for him to kiss her? "So you've said before."

"It won't happen again, Jenny. I want you to come back, and I promise I'll keep my distance." For both their sakes, Blake thought. She still wasn't looking at him, and she held herself stiff and unyielding.

He regretted touching her, Jenny realized. She wouldn't let him see how much that hurt. "Fine."

Evidently that was what she wanted to hear. At least now he knew where they stood. Blake decided to move to a safer subject. "Will you tell me what upset you before we ... went outside?"

Jenny swallowed a lump of shame. "I didn't make a list because I can't read or write. I ... I'm not retarded, but I have a learning disability."

That was one he hadn't thought of. He was surprised, but not shocked. And not convinced. "But we've talked about books and authors. And your command of the English language is better than mine."

She kept her eyes on the clouds overhead. "Aunt Moira brought home recorded books from the library and I listened to them, many over and over. Fortunately I've got a good memory. She was also an English major and she kept correcting me until I memorized the do's and don'ts. And there's television. So much can be learned from television, and you don't have to write a thing, just listen."

Despite her calm recital, he could see she was still upset. Angling on the swing, he cupped her chin, tilting her face toward him until she had no choice but to meet his eyes. "This isn't an insurmountable problem, and it's nothing to be ashamed of." He could imagine that with an ailing mother and a workaholic father they hadn't looked into solutions when she was a child. And her aunt, being in a new country, didn't know how to go about finding help. "Education's come a long way since you were a child. There are tests you can take and . . ."

Jenny shook her head. "I've *been* tested, *many* times. My father has money, you know. It was awful. One doctor after another diagnosed me as spoiled, with antisocial behavior and a phobia about schooling. It's just not something I'd go through again."

Blake stubbornly persisted. "But you play the piano by ear. You've memorized whole operas. That takes intelligence. I don't understand. Were you afraid to go to school?"

"Yes. Kindergarten, I remember, was fun. I even managed first grade all right. But then we started writing and I couldn't keep up. The teacher would get annoyed and the kids made fun of me. At home my father insisted I keep going back, that if I just concentrated, I'd get it. But I couldn't. We had terrible yelling sessions and I'd have stomachaches all the time. I started wetting the bed, and then that upset him. I couldn't seem to please anyone except my mother."

"What did she do?"

"She convinced my father to let her take me out of school so she could teach me at home. She would read to me and I would memorize the simple stories easily."

"Did that fool your father into thinking you could read?"

Jenny sighed deeply. "He just wanted peace, really. As long as we weren't quarreling, he paid little attention. My mother pacified him and he went about his business."

"Did the school authorities let you drop out without questioning?"

"We'd just moved. Father had this big house built and it was in a different school district. My records must have fallen between the cracks, because no one ever came to check on me, at least I never heard about anyone."

"What about your aunt? She was living with you then, too?"

"Yes. She always told me I was smart, but that something inside me gets confused and stops me from learning the way other people do. She devoted a lot of time to making sure I listened to the recorded books, and then we'd discuss them until I understood. And she taught me about opera and the theater and even ballet. She never once made me feel stupid the way... the way Jocelyn did."

"She's your stepmother?"

Jenny nodded. "She found out about another aunt still in Ireland—my mother and aunt's sister—who's mentally retarded. Jocelyn insisted I was, too, and she suggested to my father that I be institutionalized where I'd be with other children who were like me. That's when Aunt Moira decided we should leave."

The memory brought obvious pain to her face. Despite his previous resolution not to touch her, Blake slid his arm along the back of the swing and placed a hand on her shoulder. "You're *not* retarded, Jenny.

You're bright and beautiful.'' He hated seeing her like this. There had to be something he could do.

Jenny let herself relax fractionally. He'd taken her news better than she'd dared hope, even saying she was bright and beautiful. She knew she was neither, but she couldn't help being pleased that he thought so.

Mind racing, Blake zeroed in on a plan. He was, after all, a teacher. Perhaps he could make a difference in Jenny's life. The idea of focusing in on something other than his own problems appealed to him enormously. But he would have to go slowly, for she was convinced she couldn't learn.

"Can you really remember all the things we need from the store without a list?''

"Yes. I go for Aunt Moira all the time.''

"But you can't read the labels.''

"I recognize the boxes and the cans of the things we use regularly. You'd be surprised how many have pictures on them. I usually don't have trouble with numbers or money.''

"Let's go and you can show me.''

She felt more like having another good cry than going shopping, but he was being so kind. "All right,'' Jenny said.

"You can come in with me if you want,'' Jenny said as Blake drew the car to a stop in the supermarket parking lot.

Blake shook his head. "You know it makes me uncomfortable to be out in public. Besides, you told me you can do this without forgetting a single item, so go to it.'' He handed her the money and saw her frown.

"A hundred-dollar bill? I wonder if they've ever seen one in this small town.''

"Sure they have." He reached across her to open the door. "I'll be here when you return."

Jenny shoved the money into her pocket and stepped out.

Blake slouched back in the seat and waited until she'd gone inside, then drove out of the parking lot. It took him only a few minutes in the small downtown area to locate the library. Parking near the door, he drew in a deep breath. Jenny would never know how much it took out of him to enter a public building. But because he was determined to help her, he would endure the stares. Grabbing his cane, he went inside.

The woman at the front desk had white hair and a pleasant smile. He was surprised to notice that she looked him straight in the eye and not at his bandaged face.

"I'm looking for Moira Ryan," Blake told her. "Is she working today?"

"Yes. She's in the children's section stocking shelves, I believe." The woman waved her hand in the general direction of the back, off to the left.

Thanking her, Blake made his way back. A young woman sat studying at a table near the children's section, keeping her eye on a child of about five who was seated on the floor looking through a picture book. A short, middle-aged woman, her auburn hair caught in a bun at the nape of her neck, was restocking a shelf from a full pushcart. At his approach she turned.

"May I help you?" Moira Ryan took a closer look, then smiled. "You'd be the captain renting the Weber Cottage. Am I right?"

"Yes, Miss Ryan." Blake glanced around at the small chairs, the low bookcases, feeling large and out of place. "I was wondering if you'd have time to talk with me. I won't keep you long."

Moira removed her glasses and indicated a wooden table and chairs across the room. "We're not busy right now. Jenny's all right, isn't she?"

Blake sat down across from the chair she took. "She's fine. I left her at the supermarket. I can't believe she's able to keep a long list of grocery items in her head and not forget a one."

Folding her small hands on the tabletop, Moira studied him. "Jenny's an amazing girl. What did you want to see me about, Captain?"

"Call me Blake, please. I just learned today that Jenny can't read. I want to help her."

The clear blue eyes remained steady on his. "I see. And how did you plan to do that?"

"I have a teaching degree." His gaze roamed to the shelves lined with books. "I thought I'd check out a couple of books and try to teach her."

Moira allowed herself a small smile. "Would you be thinking it's that easy? If it were, wouldn't you think I'd have done that long ago?"

"I'm not saying it'll be easy. And I respect your feelings for your niece and your efforts on her behalf. But I'd like to try."

"You're welcome to try, but it will likely only frustrate Jenny. Has she agreed to your help?"

"I thought I'd surprise her."

"Did you now? I think you'll be the one surprised." She leaned forward, looking anxious to convince him. "Jenny is bright and intelligent. Did you know she was saying her first words when she was but six months old? By two she could sing all the *Sesame Street* songs by heart. But something goes wrong in the transmission of the written word from her eye to her brain. I've heard there are millions of learning disabled people in the world, so she's not alone.''

Blake, too, leaned forward. "She doesn't fit the description of the learning disabled. I'm not quite sure what's wrong. Have her eyes been tested?"

"Aye, and her ears, too, as well as all the rest of her. Her mother was still alive when all this came to light, and Annie took Jenny to one doctor after another. About the only thing they found wrong was that she has trouble knowing right from left."

"Directional confusion. Yes, I've heard some children have that. But most outgrow it. When was the last time Jenny was tested?"

"Oh, it's been a long while now." Moira removed a tissue from her skirt pocket and used it to polish her glasses.

"I know how quick, how smart she is, and I hate to see the world of books denied her."

"Would that be your only interest in my niece, then?"

Blake found himself shifting uneasily in his chair under the woman's clear-eyed scrutiny. Like Jenny, Moira Ryan appeared unaware of his infirmities, yet somehow seemed able to look into his mind. "Jenny's been very good to me, at a time when I've felt very low. She won't let me feel sorry for myself. She's kind and generous with her time and..."

"And?"

Blake cleared his throat. "And I want to do this for her. I have no ulterior motives, if that's what you mean."

Moira took her time putting her rimless glasses back on. "I think you should know, Captain, that Jenny's not very experienced in the ways of the world. Or of men. She's been quite sheltered, and I wouldn't want someone to take advantage of her trusting nature and her innocence.''

Innocence. He wondered if she meant that in the broad sense, or if her aunt was saying that Jenny was untouched. A little unusual for a woman of twenty-five, yet he'd felt that about her from the beginning. "Nor would I, Miss Ryan."

The little woman's perceptive blue eyes studied him for a long moment, then she nodded. "Then we understand each other. You seem like a good and decent man, and I know Jenny's fond of you."

Blake raised a surprised eyebrow. "She told you that?"

"She didn't need to." Moira rose. "If you're intent on trying, I can recommend several books. But I warn you, you may upset her."

"I'll be careful not to upset her."

"All right then. Let me get the books and check them out for you."

At the front desk she arranged for a library card for him, stamped the books and handed them to him. "It was good meeting you, Captain," Moira said with a guarded smile.

Blake reached to shake her hand, finding he liked Moira Ryan more than he had thought he would. "The pleasure was mine." Walking to the car, he checked his watch. He would have to hurry if he was to get back to the store parking lot before Jenny came out.

They were laughing. It had to do with the silly lyrics from an old Irish song that Jenny had been trying to teach Blake as they drove home. He had deliberately turned the words around, changing their meaning, because he loved to hear her laugh. He'd coaxed her into the playful mood, anxious to put behind them the morning's bad beginning.

If he hadn't been so occupied with watching her as she struggled through a fit of the giggles, he probably would have noticed the car parked in his driveway from the road instead of when he pulled up behind it.

Sobering quickly, he studied the rental plates, then heard his name called from the direction of the front porch. A tall man with short blond hair, wearing a lieutenant's uniform and a nervous smile, got up from the steps and stood looking toward them.

Slowly Blake got out of the car. "Tom, how are you?"

"That's my line," Tom Payne said as he walked over. His looks were all-American, his handshake firm.

"I'm getting by. What brings you to this part of the world?"

"Can't a man stop by to see a friend?" Tom's eyes shifted to the woman who'd come alongside Blake, and he didn't bother to hide his curiosity.

Blake stepped back to include her. "Jenny, meet Lieutenant Tom Payne. Tom, this is Jenny Starbuck."

Tom's big hand swallowed her small one as he greeted her. "Good to know you."

"Yes, you, too." Jenny turned to remove a grocery bag from the back seat. "I'll just put these away and get some iced tea," she said, giving Blake a quick glance. She could see he was uneasy with his visitor.

"Let me help." Tom quickly grabbed the other two sacks and followed Jenny as she hurried through the gate.

Blake walked after, wondering who'd sent Tom to check up on him and why. Tom was big and blond and bursting with good health, Blake noted as he held open the screen door.

"Nice little place," Tom said as he set the bags on the table and sent a smile Jenny's way.

"Let's go sit out back," Blake suggested, leading the way. He'd forgotten his cane in the car and now found, much to his dismay, that he was limping more than usual. To hell with it, he thought as he eased into his usual lounge chair.

Tom chose a straight chair, propping an ankle on his knee and looking the yard over, then lifting his gaze past the shrubs to the sea. "I love the ocean. You do much swimming?"

"No. Where are you staying?"

"At Homestead Air Base. Just got transferred last week." Tom angled round so he could look at Blake. "How are you *really* doing?"

Blake shrugged. "Some days are better than others." He respected Tom Payne, knew him to be a good pilot and a nice guy. Of all the pilots he'd trained, he supposed he liked Tom the best, though he'd never had time to get to know many of the students very well. Tom had visited him at Brooks a couple of times after the accident, looking more uncomfortable each time. The guilt of the survivor, Blake guessed. The experiences they'd shared back at Selfridge seemed like a hundred years ago to Blake. And he wasn't sure he wanted to sit around reminiscing. "Did they tell you to look me up?"

Tom colored slightly. "Not exactly." He dug into his pocket and pulled out a brown case. "They did ask me to give you this."

Blake took the box and flipped it open. A set of gold oak leaves glistened in a weak sun as he looked them over.

"Congratulations, Major," Tom said, his voice young and sincere. "You deserve far more than that in my book."

He had known they were coming, though he hadn't guessed the brass would have them hand-delivered. "The paperwork came through on the promotion before I left." He flipped the case closed. "Thanks."

"That makes you one of the youngest majors in the air force, right? Quite an honor."

"They can keep the honors. I'd rather be back flying."

"Well, maybe one day, after a little more surgery..."

Blake let out a noisy sigh. "So you talked with Dr. Ambrose, too." It wasn't a question.

Tom shifted in his seat. "When he learned I was heading this way, he asked if I'd try to persuade you to think about returning for that surgery. He has your best interests at heart, Blake."

Blake sent a frown in the direction of the sea. "Yeah, everyone's got my best interests at heart."

Seemingly anxious to change the subject, Tom nodded toward the house. "Your girl, Jenny. She seems real nice."

Blake frowned. "She's my housekeeper, not my girl."

"No kidding? Awfully young for a housekeeper. You seemed to be having fun with her when you drove up. You should see the woman who keeps house for my mother. Hardly good-looking. And no personality."

Blake couldn't help thinking he'd have been a lot better off with that kind of housekeeper. The screen door slammed, and he looked up to see Jenny coming toward them carrying a tray.

Like the gentleman he was, Tom jumped to his feet and hurried to help her. "That looks terrific," he told her as he set the tray on the small wooden table. Pulling up a third chair, he held it out for her. "Please join us."

Uncertainly she looked at Blake, who nodded, but she still felt uneasy as she sat down.

"So, Jenny, do you live around here?"

"Yes, not far." She sipped her tea, wondering why the air seemed heavy with tension.

"Blake, show her what I brought. The air force has promoted him to major. I brought his oak leaves."

Blake handed her the box without comment.

Jenny examined the oak leaves, impressed. "Congratulations," she told Blake, but he was frowning up at the sky.

"Looks like we're in for a summer shower." Blake pushed to his feet. Tom had come a long way and, though he didn't feel much like entertaining, he could at least be civil. "Is there enough chicken for all of us if we invite the lieutenant for dinner, Jenny?" With her there the conversation should go more easily.

Jenny brightened, thinking Blake's mood had shifted for the better. "Yes, plenty." She gathered up the glasses.

"Thanks, that'd be great." As the first of the raindrops fell, Tom followed them into the cottage.

* * *

The two men were deep in a discussion on the merits of several of the newer jet planes versus the older models as they ate dinner. A slow, steady rain fell outside as Jenny listened quietly, watching her companions from under lowered lashes.

Tom Payne was classically handsome, yet his face looked boyish and unformed alongside Blake's. His blond hair was cut very short. She much preferred Blake's shaggy length. The lieutenant's summer uniform fit very nicely. She couldn't help but wonder what Blake would look like in his. Suppressing a sigh, she realized she'd probably never know.

As Jenny passed the chicken to Tom, she caught Blake's serious gray eyes watching her. He seemed less tense, but still guarded, and she wondered what he was thinking. Perhaps she shouldn't have accepted his invitation to remain for dinner. As he continued to stare, she dropped her gaze, suddenly remembering the kisses they'd shared that morning all too vividly.

"Did you know that Blake saved my life?" Tom asked, turning to Jenny. At her surprised glance he nodded. "I was the student pilot in the plane that went down. When I realized we were going to crash, I just froze, couldn't move. Blake ejected me." His tone was respectful; his glance toward his former instructor bordered on worship.

Jenny swung her eyes to Blake. "I didn't know."

"Then he managed to turn the plane so that it hit an empty field. Just missed a whole section of houses. It was in all the papers."

Embarrassed more by the way Jenny was looking at him than at Tom's words, Blake made a dismissive gesture. "That was a long time ago."

"Maybe so," Tom continued. "But I'll never forget it. So you're working for a genuine hero, Jenny."

She sensed Blake's unease and turned to smile at Tom. "I'm not surprised."

Blake watched the two of them, both tan and beautiful, and felt a rush of jealousy that stunned him. Only this morning he'd lectured himself on backing off from Jenny.

"This dinner's wonderful, Jenny," Tom told her. "Blake, if you eat like this every night, you're a lucky man."

"Come on, Tom," Blake said, suddenly no longer hungry. "Your wife's a good cook, isn't she?" Now why had he felt it necessary to inform Jenny that Tom was married? Gritting his teeth, Blake decided he knew the reason, and it didn't please him.

"Yes, Laura's a great cook. I really miss her." Finished, Tom shoved his plate aside. "When I got transferred, she decided to stay home, since we don't know how long I'll be here. It gets pretty lonely for both of us."

A sudden gust of wind sent the rain pounding against the window. Jenny frowned as she rose to clear the table. "I should have gone home earlier."

"Leave the dishes," Blake told her, rising. "I'll drive you home."

"No need for you to go out in the rain," Tom said as he stood. "I have to get going myself. I'll be glad to take you home, Jenny."

Blake picked up his keys. "It's out of your way."

Tom touched Blake's arm. "It's no trouble, really." He held out his hand. "Good to see you, Blake. And thanks for dinner."

Jenny had watched the play between them and decided it would be best if she stayed out of the discussion. She didn't care who took her home at this point, but she desperately wanted to leave. It had been a long, unsettling day and the tension was back.

Hiding his annoyance, Blake gave in. Shaking hands with Tom, he even found a small smile. "Thanks for coming by."

"I'll see you tomorrow," Jenny said, but Blake was already opening the door for them, avoiding her eyes.

Tom took her arm and hurried her through the rain to his rented car.

For a long while Blake stood on the porch and gazed out at the dismal evening. He struggled with a kaleidoscope of emotions. He wanted to be left alone, yet when Jenny was gone, he felt lonely. It didn't make sense, yet there it was.

With a determined grimace he fought to bring forth his protective anger. He didn't need a woman in his life. Not Eleanor, not Jenny, not anyone.

He didn't give a damn if she was attracted to all the Toms of the world. He would treat her like a sister, focus on teaching her, helping her. And he would *not*, by God, let himself care for her or any other woman ever again. It was the only way to avoid being hurt, to avoid these debilitating bouts of jealousy, of rejection. No one could hurt him if he didn't care.

That decided, Blake went inside.

Chapter Six

The thing to do was to approach her correctly, Blake told himself as he examined the books he'd borrowed from the library. Jenny was in the kitchen ironing. He would wait until she finished, then he would call her over.

She hadn't been to the cottage for the past two days; Dr. Swain had needed her. After their uneasy parting the last time, Blake had been rather glad to have the break. It gave him time to think out his plan to teach her to read. Still, he had missed her and was glad she'd returned this morning.

Perhaps he would make it seem as if she'd be doing him a big favor by letting him help her, that he was thinking about returning to teaching after his convalescence and needed the practice. Yes, that was the way to go about it. Pleased with the thought, he sat back on the couch and waited.

Twenty minutes later as she passed by, he took her hand and patted the seat beside him. "Come sit with me a minute."

With a questioning look in her eyes Jenny sat down.

Blake cleared his throat. "Do you recall the other day when we talked about your not being able to read?"

Instantly her expression changed, growing wary. "Yes."

"I told you I wanted to help and I do. I used to be a fairly good teacher. Will you let me see if there's anything I can do?"

Jenny moved back, leaving more space between them. "I don't want to do this, Blake," she said softly.

"You don't want to know how to read?"

"Of course I do. But I've learned to accept that I can't be taught. Why can't you accept that, too?"

"Because I'm pigheaded and stubborn."

She almost smiled. "Yes, you are."

"Won't you try, for me?"

She wanted to please him, but he didn't know what he was asking of her. It wasn't just the reading; it was the memories the effort brought back. With a trembling hand she took the book from him and opened it.

Scooting closer, encouraged by her apparent cooperation, Blake turned the pages. "This is a primer and it begins by explaining the alphabet."

Jenny's hand clenched into a fist in her lap. "I know the alphabet."

"I don't mean to insult you, Jenny. I'm trying to discover what you know and don't know."

Using her index finger, she pointed. "This is an *A*, this is a *B*, this is a *C*. You want me to go on?"

"No, no." He flipped several pages. "Read me the top line."

She swallowed hard. "I can't. It's just a bunch of letters that don't make sense to me."

Patiently he turned to another section. "Try this then."

"I told you I know my numbers. One, two, three, five, four..."

"Four, five."

"All right, four, five." Deliberately she closed the book. "I don't want to do this." Rising, she walked back to the kitchen.

Taking a deep breath, Blake followed her. She stood at the sink, staring out the window, her back to him. Hating the fact that he'd upset her, he slid his hands along her arms and pulled her body back to lean against his. A gesture of comfort, he told himself. "It's all right."

She held herself stiff, tense. She didn't see the backyard leading into the woods. She saw instead Jocelyn Starbuck's triumphant smile as she turned to Lucius, having just reduced Jenny to tears over another reading lesson. "You see, darling. Nearly nine and she can't read the simplest book and can't be taught. She's retarded. You must learn to accept it. Why not send her where she can be with children who are like she is, where she won't feel stupid and inadequate?" Jenny shuddered at the memory, fighting against its grip on her.

"I feel so dumb," she whispered.

"You're *not* dumb." Blake rubbed her arms, letting her know with his touch what he couldn't seem to convince her of with words. "I believe in you. I believe there's a way."

She turned to face him, remaining in the circle of his arms. "Why are you persisting in this?"

"Because I want you to be happy."

"I *am* happy. Or I was until you started all this."

"I feel like you're missing so much. There's a whole world out there, waiting for you to discover it. And the key is reading, education, travel."

"That's the same world you've turned away from by coming to this isolated cottage and hiding behind that bandage. Why do you want to change me? I haven't tried to change you."

She had him there. But it wasn't the same thing, Blake decided. "All right, I'll drop it." For now, he silently added.

He held her loosely, staring out the window. There had to be a way.

"Your leg is healed," Chet Ambrose said as he ran his fingers along Blake's left shank. "These thicker keloid scars will lighten and soften in time. All the skin transplants took as far as I can see."

"The problem is the knee," Blake reluctantly admitted. "If I walk too long, or sit in one position too long."

Chet nodded. "Then it hurts. I know. Some of that may never go away entirely. The problem, as you're well aware, has to do with the replaced shattered bone. They did the best they could at the time, considering all your other injuries, but this leg is still shorter than the other. Which is one reason why your limp persists."

Blake eased into a sitting position on the examining table. "I could live with the limp if it wasn't so damn painful."

"It's painful because you're putting strain on the knee. That whole kneecap's been rebuilt. It simply can't handle the pressure. We've tried lifts in your shoes and that hasn't solved the problem. You need another bone transplant—a metal plate in there, if necessary—to make the left leg the same length as your right. When that heals, your limp will probably disappear. And without that strain, the pain in your knee will ease."

"*Probably*, you say. No guarantees, right?"

Chet stuck his hands into the pockets of his white lab coat. "You should know by now that when it comes to the human body, especially a *damaged* human body, there are never guarantees. But my best educated guess is that the procedure I've outlined, which is the one my brother told you you'd one day be facing, will take care of your problem."

Blake scooted off the table and reached for his pants. "*Probably* isn't good enough, Chet. They'll get in there and find something else—an atrophied muscle, accumulated scar tissue, something—and tell me I'll need still another operation." He buttoned his slacks. "I think I'll take my chances with Mother Nature."

"Take a look at your X ray," Chet said, pointing to the illuminated viewing screen on his wall. "This problem isn't going to go away. It will probably get worse without surgery."

Slipping on his shoes, Blake smiled. "There's that word *probably* again."

"Damn it, man, you're only thirty-two. If you let this go, you'll be a cripple by forty."

"I'm a cripple now, Chet." Blake's mouth was grim. "I don't want any more surgery."

Chet flicked off the light and removed the X ray. "Have it your way. No one can force you to become whole again. You have to want it badly enough."

Blake banked his rush of anger, knowing that Chet Ambrose was only doing what a good doctor should do, explaining to his patient all his options. That didn't mean the patient had to like what he heard. Want it badly? Hell, yes, he did. If the medics could offer him more than nebulous *probablies,* he'd undoubtedly go for it. But no one knew better than he that bone surgery was very painful, the recovery period long. All that for a *maybe?* No thanks, he thought.

"All right, let me check your face." Chet motioned Blake to the chair. Removing the bandage, he examined the area beneath it with skilled fingers. "This, too, is healed. But you already know that, don't you? And still you cover it up when there's no need."

"I don't want to risk infection."

Chet stepped back and leaned a hip against the edge of the examining table. "Why are you hiding, Blake? You told me when you arrived that you'd talked with the army shrink and he told you that part of the healing process was learning to accept the changes in your body."

Blake ran a hand through his hair, uncomfortably aware that Chet's words were true. "Yeah, well, that's easier said than done. You don't have to face a world that's repulsed by the sight of you."

"If you can't accept how you look, how can you expect others to?"

"I don't expect anything from anyone." Blake stood, needing to leave, to get some air. "Is that all?"

Chet let out a discouraged sigh, then clapped a hand on Blake's broad shoulder. "I hate to keep at you. But I wish you'd at least talk with a plastic surgeon. They can do so much today."

"I'll give it some thought." He turned, feeling his anger drain. "I don't mean to take my frustrations out on you."

"I know. Call me if you need anything."

He remembered the major reason he'd forced himself to visit the doctor. "There is something. Are you aware that Jenny Starbuck can't read?"

Chet nodded. "Yes. Moira told me long ago when they first moved here. I understand she's been seen by nearly every specialist in the state."

"All that was years ago. I've tried to help her myself, but she only gets frustrated and angry. I was wondering if you knew of a therapist who specialized in learning disabilities. Maybe it's not a medical disorder but rather a perception problem."

"There's a woman who works through the school system, I believe. I'll have my receptionist get you her name." Chet started toward his front office. "Don't expect miracles, though. I know they've tried just about everything."

In a few minutes Chet handed Blake a card. "Here it is, Roberta Ames. I remember now. She's very good."

Blake slipped the card into his pocket. "I appreciate this."

"Would I be out of line if I asked why you're so interested in helping Jenny Starbuck?"

Blake shrugged. "Why not? I have the time. And didn't you say it would be good for me to think about something other than myself?"

Chet smiled. "So I did. Good luck."

With a nod Blake left the office, anxious to get back to the cottage and Jenny. He scarcely noticed that his limp wasn't nearly as pronounced leaving as when he walked in.

"I'm calling about a friend, Miss Ames," Blake said into the phone. "My name is Blake Hanley. Dr. Chet Ambrose gave me your number."

"Yes, Dr. Ambrose has referred an occasional child to me. What can I do for you?"

"I have an adult friend who can't read."

"Is your friend a foreigner perhaps?"

He liked her voice, calm and patient. "She was born in Ireland but raised here. Her English is very good. I understand that she was tested extensively as a child and diagnosed as having directional confusion, antisocial behavior and school phobia. Physically they found nothing wrong with her."

"She's healthy in every other way?"

"Very, and quite bright, I might add. She's got a fantastic memory and only has to hear a melody once to be able to play it on the piano."

"But she can't read. Interesting." Roberta Ames paused. "Has she ever been evaluated by a learning disability instructor?"

Blake kept his voice low and his eye on the closed door of his den. He could hear Jenny vacuuming in his bedroom and hoped to end his call before she finished. "I'm not sure. If she has, it's been many years ago. I'm calling to ask if you'd see her."

"Has she had an IQ test?"

"I don't know. I'd wager she has a high IQ but would test poorly unless the questions were read to her and explained."

"Yes, I've often done that. Your friend interests me, Mr. Hanley. Tell me, does she ever have difficulty with her balance?"

Blake could recall only one incident—the day Jenny had fallen in the kitchen. "She might have. Do you have something in mind?"

"Perhaps. Of course, I'd need to test her. Did she ever have a severe ear infection as a child, do you know?"

"I don't, but I'll find out."

"Fine. Would you like an appointment?"

"Yes, but I'll have to phone you back. I have to persuade her to see you first."

"She's reluctant to learn?"

"She's been convinced by others that she can't. But I know she's quick and intelligent, and I want others to know it, too. Most of all, I want *her* to realize it."

"Call back when you've convinced her to see me, Mr. Hanley."

"Thank you, I will." Slowly Blake put the phone down. He was simply doing what any good friend would do for another, he told himself. Nothing out of the ordinary.

Shifting his gaze, he stared out the window at the distant sea. Perhaps he did care for Jenny Starbuck. But it was a friendly caring, the kind that had nowhere to go except toward separation.

The best thing he could do for Jenny would be to open up the world of books and reading to her, then let her go, let her find someone who would appreciate her beauty and her eager mind. Leaning back in his chair, Blake closed his eyes and tried to conjure up brotherly feelings, instead of the more disturbing ones that kept him awake nights.

"I don't swim." Blake's mouth formed a thin, stubborn line.

"Of course you do," Jenny told him, her smile daring him to disagree. She stood with her hands on her hips, looking down at him as he lazed back in his easy chair. "You've already told me that back in Michigan you used to play tennis, hunt and swim. Now don't be denying it." From behind her back she whipped out a pair of swim trunks. "I found these in your drawer when I was putting away your laundry. Come on. You're getting fat and lazy always sitting around in your chair."

"Need I remind you that I'm here recuperating from an accident?"

She shook her head at him. "I love it when you resort to your captain-in-command voice. Blake, you forget that *I* talk with Dr. Ambrose, too. You need exercise, and swimming's the kind that'll do you the least harm." She took hold of his hand. "Get up now."

He made one last-ditch effort. "I don't pay you to go swimming. I pay you to—"

"I know. To clean your house, do your laundry, fix your dinner. All finished, your lordship. It's four o'clock and I'll thank you not to be bossing me about on my own time."

How easily she could charm him. "Funny how your brogue thickens when you get excited. You sound just like your aunt."

Jenny's eyes widened. "And when were you talking with Aunt Moira?"

"At the library when I checked out the books you won't let me help you with."

"Odd that she didn't mention your visit."

He saw an opportunity and moved in. "Let's make a deal. We study one hour, then swim one hour."

She dropped his hand. "You'll be striking no deals with me, Blake Hanley. If you intend to be stubborn, to sit here and rot away in that chair while the sun and the sea are so glorious, then I'll go swim alone."

Damn, but she knew how to get to him. "Wait." He let his eyes roam up and down her suggestively. "Since you don't have a bathing suit, I assume you'll be skinny-dipping, right?"

"You assume incorrectly." Nevertheless, she felt herself growing pink at the thought. "I brought my suit this morning, hoping to persuade you. Are you coming or not?"

Perhaps it was her sense of playfulness after a week of watching her go about her work, subdued and quiet. But more likely it was the mental picture of her running into the waves wearing only a skimpy bathing suit that had him rising out of his chair. "Can I just go down to the beach and watch you? I…I'm not crazy about letting the world see the scarred wreck I've become."

At the doorway she turned back to him. Her voice softened; she knew that at last he'd voiced his real reason. "There'll be no one there but you and me. And to my eyes your body's beautiful."

She left then, and in a moment he heard the door to the bathroom close. His body beautiful? She truly was the most amazing woman.

Carrying his suit, he walked to his bedroom to change.

"Last one in's a monkey's uncle," Jenny called over her shoulder as she dropped her towel on the warm sand. Breaking into a run, she rushed to meet an on-coming wave. Wading farther out, she dived into a swirl of water.

Blake slipped off his shirt, tossing it next to her towel, and stood watching her. She was being consid-erate, he knew, letting him remove his pants in pri-vacy and walk into the water at his own pace. For a long moment he gazed at her floating in on a wave, then hurtling back to catch another. Lord, but she was beautiful.

He'd thought of her as almost too slender, but re-alized now that it was because she always wore loose clothing. The black one-piece suit molded to her curves, revealing the fullness of her breasts and the sweet flare of her hips. It had been a very long time since he'd looked at a woman and felt the unmistak-able stirring of desire that Jenny had been able to bring about in him so effortlessly. Watching her laugh up at the blue sky, tossing her long silken hair back as she spun about, it was impossible not to feel her magnetism.

He had worried that the passion had been burned out of him by the same flames that had damaged his skin. But he'd been wrong. A sweet, innocent woman had brought him back to life. Of course, it was mainly physical, though he honestly liked Jenny. Still, he wanted no involvement, and she deserved a man with a better future than he could offer. Sliding off his white jeans, Blake wandered into the foamy waves.

Face pointed upward, Jenny rose from under the sea, letting the water drip off her long hair. Knees bent, she stood on the sandy bottom, watching Blake hurry in until he was up to his waist, then walk toward her more slowly. She was quite a distance out, for the ocean at this point deepened gradually. Blinking moisture from her eyes, she watched his slow progress.

She'd allowed him the privacy to disrobe, wishing he hadn't felt the need. With rest and good food his body had regained some of the weight he'd lost, she'd been noticing. His shoulders were wide, his arms muscular, his chest firm and his stomach hard and flat. She had told him the truth when she said that he was beautiful in her eyes. The pity was that he would never believe her. Though she knew she shouldn't, she was unable to stop wanting him, even when he didn't want her. Even when he turned from her whenever he felt himself drawing closer.

A dozen yards away he ducked under, emerging very near her moments later. She smiled as he tossed back his wet hair. "I think I should cut your hair. It's getting nearly as long as mine."

He stood with knees bent, his arms swirling the water at his sides. "Is there no end to your talent?"

"Well, I can't walk on water." She gave him an impish grin.

He moved closer, drawn, despite his best efforts to remain unaffected. He stretched his arm to trail his fingers through her hair, floating on the surface. "You have beautiful hair."

"Thank you, kind sir. Now how about a race?"

Swimming he could probably beat her, whereas walking he hadn't a chance. "You're on. Where to?"

"To that buoy out there, all right?"

"Okay." He stood up as she did. "On three. One, two, three!" Blake struck out with a fast side stroke. Unable to push off as smoothly as she, he was behind at first but soon passed her easily. The waves weren't rough; the sea, fairly calm, offered no problems.

She wasn't far behind him, he could tell. She'd been right to coax him out. It felt good to stretch his limbs, to feel the gentle support of the water yet glide through it. He'd thought the saltwater might sting his cheek, but it didn't bother him. Maybe he should swim a little every day, get more sun, try to build his body slowly back to what it had been.

At the buoy he swung around and found her only two lengths behind him. Laughing, he reached for her hand. "Not bad for a girl."

"Hey, fella," she said. "Some of the best swimmers in the world are mere girls." Treading water, she smiled at him. "Nicer than you'd thought out here, eh?"

"Yes." But treading water would probably wear out his leg too fast. "Let's go back in a ways where we can stand." He opted for a leisurely breaststroke on the return trip, and Jenny kept up with him. Finally able to stand, Blake set his feet wide apart in the shifting sand.

Coming up behind him, Jenny touched his shoulders. Then, on impulse, she bent her head to kiss a small scar on his upper arm.

Stunned, he swiveled around, his hand going to the spot she'd kissed. "I...doesn't it bother you, all these marks on me?"

"No, why should it?" She drifted closer. "It's what's inside a package that counts, not the wrappings. My mother used to say that. Do you judge a person by how they look?''

She had brought him up short again. He wasn't sure how to answer her, so he didn't. ''You continue to astound me,'' he said, holding on to her hands.

A wave moved in suddenly, shifting them again. Jenny's feet couldn't quite reach bottom. Lightly floating and feeling bold, she dared move nearer to him. Laying her arm on his shoulder, her hand moved to the back of his neck and into his hair. She tried to think of something light, something funny to say. But the buoyancy of the saltwater brought her even closer up against his body. When his arm went around to steady her and her breasts touched his chest, she forgot wanting to say anything.

Blake saw her eyes turn dark and slumberous, and he could fight his feelings no longer. His mouth touched hers, his one hand tangling in her hair while the other pressed against the smooth skin of her back. Her lips moved over his, then opened for the entry of his tongue. The scent of the sea mixed with the heat of the sun and the sweet aroma of the woman who was suddenly pliant and yielding in his arms.

Was that the ocean roaring in his ears, or was that the sound of blood rushing through his veins? He plunged her deeper into the kiss, needing to discover more of her. His senses sharpened and he felt alive, more alive than he'd felt in months. With the help of the sea he could hold her easily, and he did so with a fierce pleasure. Lowering his hand, he guided her legs to wrap around his waist, anchoring her to him. Then he returned his attention to her marvelous mouth.

This was even more exciting than the first time he'd kissed her, Jenny thought. And it was nothing like anything she'd ever known or dreamed about. She felt as if she'd been pulled into the eye of a storm as her will melted under its force. She could feel Blake's strength as he gripped her to him, his hands roaming her back and trailing heat wherever they touched.

For the first time in her life she felt the wonderfully aching needs of a woman, starting in her center and spreading to every part of her being. Shamelessly she returned his kiss with all the passion she'd been saving for the one man who would set her free. She could see nothing, hear nothing, feel nothing; she knew only savage desire for this man. She opened her eyes and searched his.

They were pewter-gray and filled with the same unanswered yearning that clawed at her. She stared back at him, scarcely able to believe he could want her, too. "Are you going to pull away from me again?" she asked, her voice husky.

"I wish I could."

"The other day, when you kissed me, it was the first time for me." She watched his eyes widen in surprise.

"You can't be serious. There had to have been boys, men, dates."

Jenny shook her head. "I never wanted to until I met you."

Why did that please him so much? Did he really want so desperately to believe it, despite his declarations to the contrary? He felt her tremble in his arms and tightened his hold on her. "Don't be afraid."

"I'm not. I just never knew I could feel like this."

He smiled then and raised a hand to touch her cheek. "It's taken me a little by surprise, too." A wave rushed by, nearly knocking him over, but he clutched her to him. "As far as kissing goes, I think you're a quick study."

But Jenny didn't smile, still adjusting to what her body was feeling. "It's not like this with everyone, is it?"

Blake shook his head, then grabbed her again as a large wave came crashing into them. When they bounced up out of the water and he shook his hair back, he saw that one strap of her suit had drifted off her shoulder. His eyes, hot and hungry, darted to hers.

Jenny watched him while her heart pounded against her ribs. She had never wanted like this before—her head spinning, her blood racing. Yet she didn't even know what exactly it was she wanted.

Blake felt as if they were the only two people in the world. The sun behind her head was an orange ball beginning its slow descent; its color haloed her and sprinkled gold on her hair. The water slapped against his waist, but the waves were calmer now. Feet anchored in the sand, he felt strong and solid and filled with desire for her. But he couldn't take advantage of the innocence her aunt had warned him about. Regretfully he touched her strap and slowly began to raise it back in place.

But Jenny moved her hand to stop his. Water beaded on his hair and slid down to drip on his broad shoulders. The ache of need throbbed through her. "Please, Blake. You make me feel things I've never even imagined. Don't push me away again."

He would have walked away from his own need. But what he saw in her eyes had him captivated. Slowly he slid her strap lower, her hand still on his. With a quick movement of her shoulders the other strap dropped free and drifted down. Blake's breath caught in his throat as she bared herself to him.

"So beautiful," he whispered as his fingers closed over her suddenly swelling flesh. She was cool and firm and fitted wonderfully within his palms. Her breathing was becoming labored, as was his. Shifting his hands to her back, he lifted her to his waiting mouth. His lips teased and caressed her breast, then closed over the rosy peak. She arched her back and sighed deeply, her hands going to the back of his head. He moved to the other side, and Jenny pressed him closer, her head falling back and her eyes fluttering closed.

For long moments they stood like that until Blake could no longer ignore the painful reaction of his body. Easing her back from him, he reluctantly covered her nakedness. He'd been the first man to see her, to kiss and arouse her. At least he'd have that to remember. "We have to go back."

She didn't move. "Are you sorry you touched me?" she asked.

"Never. Are you?"

"No. I trust you." She wanted to say more, much more, but her inexperience stopped her. Men probably didn't like forward women. They preferred to lead the way. She would be patient.

He took her hand and started back toward shore. He didn't deserve her trust, not when all he wanted to do was lie down in the warm sand with her and bury himself inside her.

What, he asked himself, was he going to do about Jenny Starbuck?

Chapter Seven

The phone rang as Jenny slipped the key into her back door. Thinking it was probably Aunt Moira calling to say she'd be working late again, she hurried to answer. But the voice that greeted her was deep and resonant.

"Jenny girl, how are you these days?" Lucius Starbuck asked.

Taken aback, Jenny dragged the phone cord to the table and sat down. "I'm well, Father. How are you?"

"Good, good. Working long hours as usual. Not home much, but then that's not such a sacrifice."

Was he hinting that he preferred being away from Jocelyn? Jenny wondered. Though it galled her to do it, she opted for the polite inquiry. "How is Jocelyn?"

"Very fit. She's just back from a couple of weeks at some spa or another. Can't blame her, with me being away so much."

She could hear the slight wheeze that she'd always associated with her father's breathing and pictured his full, florid face, usually damp with sweat. His white hair would likely have thinned a bit since she'd last seen him three years ago. He was probably wearing one of the white suits he had an affinity for, along with a white silk shirt and a black string tie. He'd be seated at his mammoth, leather-topped desk in his study, a cigar smoldering in his ashtray and his black Stetson somewhere nearby. The image reminded Jenny of the television westerns she used to watch. The good guys had always worn white hats.

"How's Moira?" Lucius asked into the silence.

"She's well. Not home from the library yet this evening."

"Are you still working for that vet, what's-his-name?"

"Dr. Swain. Yes, I am." Jenny felt no need to tell him of her other job and hoped he'd run out of questions soon. Though Lucius didn't phone often, his calls were unsettling.

Lucius's deep voice took on a note of reluctant concern. "You sound distracted, Jenny. Are you all right?"

"I'm fine, really. I was racing with Rafferty out back and I'm a bit out of breath, that's all."

"Uh-huh. I'm calling because I had an idea. I'll be going next week to Ireland to check on a company project. A short trip. I thought maybe you'd enjoy coming with me, visiting the little village where you were born outside Dublin. What do you say, Jenny girl?''

He'd stunned her. In all these years he'd never once asked her along on any of his many trips. She was immediately wary. ''Is Jocelyn going?''

''Well, yes. She loves traveling, you may remember. But she'd be staying in Dublin. You and I could visit your mother's people.'' He paused. ''If they're still alive, that is.''

''If you mean my grandparents, they both died some years ago. Aunt Moira kept in touch. There's only Uncle Vincent, Aunt Irene and a handful of cousins left. And, of course, Aunt Maureen.'' The flawed one, the one whose very name had made Lucius nervous and the one Jocelyn labeled retarded, despite Moira's explanation that Maureen was merely a bit slower than others.

''Yes, Maureen. Where is she now?''

''She lives with Vincent's son Patrick and his family.''

''Ah yes. So, what do you say, Jenny?''

Perhaps if Jocelyn weren't going. But no, no, she still wouldn't want to leave Blake. Not now. ''I hate to disappoint you, but I think I'd best stay home.''

''Well, it was just an impulse to ask you. Probably wasn't a good idea at that.''

He'd accepted her refusal quickly enough, Jenny thought, not quite sure why that disappointed her. Truth be known, he most likely hadn't wanted her along, anyway. His conscience, something Lucius Starbuck usually ignored, had undoubtedly made him call. He sounded almost relieved that she'd turned him down.

"Some other time perhaps," Jenny said, knowing full well that there probably would be no right time for her and the man who'd given her life.

"Sure, sure. Tell Moira I asked after her, will you?"

"Yes, I will. Have a good trip."

"Jenny?" Again that hesitant pause. "Is there anything you need?"

"Not a thing, Father." Love, perhaps, once upon a time a long while ago. She no longer even needed that from him. She'd done without his love too long to miss it anymore.

"Goodbye, Jenny. I'll be in touch."

"Goodbye, Father." Slowly Jenny hung up the phone and sat staring at the black instrument.

She felt like weeping. Not for what was, but for all that might have been. Replacing the phone on the counter, she ran her hands along her arms and hugged herself.

If only the fates would see fit that she might have a child one day, she'd give it so much love that it would never feel as she now felt. Cheated, lonely, wanting. For years she'd accepted the way she was, yet now she was restless and yearning again for all the things she'd thought she could live without. Why, suddenly, was this happening to her?

Jenny closed her eyes on the answer. Blake Hanley.

She wanted him fiercely, beside her always. Answering his needs would be the same as answering her own. He'd awakened a woman's body, but more importantly, he'd stolen a woman's heart.

Yesterday, standing in the sunlight with him as the ocean waves swirled around them, she'd admitted the truth to herself. She loved him. Could love come like that, in an instant, like a flash of lightning? Or had it been growing inside her always, like a planted seed waiting for the sun to make it bloom? Jenny didn't know. She only knew that she yearned for this man and this man only.

She felt a lone tear slide down her cheek. Why couldn't he love her, too?

"And what would you be up to now, Blake Hanley?" Jenny asked warily.

Blake stood on the porch, his car keys in hand. "I invited you for a ride. Why are you so suspicious?"

He looked boyishly appealing, and she knew that, after yesterday, he was aware she was far from immune to him. She noticed he was wearing a short-sleeved shirt for a change, allowing the world to glimpse the few scars on his left arm. But the bandage was still in place on his cheek. What could he have in mind? she wondered as she searched his eyes. "I'm a naturally suspicious woman, that's why."

He scooted Rafferty into the kitchen, pushed in the lock and pulled the door shut. "Come on. Take a chance. I think you'll like my surprise."

Reluctantly she followed him to the car. The day was a little overcast, but the afternoon sun kept dodging the clouds. She climbed into his car and, to her surprise, he turned along the beach path, not the road into town. "Are you kidnapping me? I warn you, Aunt Moira hasn't the money for a hefty ransom."

Blake glanced over at her, thinking she looked impossibly young today with her long hair twisted into a single braid that hung halfway down her back. At least when she looked like this it was easier for him to keep his mind on what he wanted to teach her and not on how he'd like to lead her into his bedroom. The very thought had him frowning in frustration.

Watching closely, Jenny saw that they were approaching a section of beach much like the Daytona Beach area where they held car races. "Are we going to an auto race?"

"Patience, patience." Blake kept his features even as he watched her struggle with her curiosity. He had relaxed the pressure on her about reading lessons lately, hoping to catch her off guard with this new ploy, but he hadn't forgotten his goal—not for a moment.

This new plan had come to him as the perfect way to make her want to learn to read. He hoped it worked. The more he kept himself focused on helping her, the more chance he had of keeping his errant mind on track. As they came around a short rise, he stopped the car and turned to her.

"Since you won't let me teach you to read, I thought you might instead like to learn to drive."

She had wanted to drive for a long time. But even in a small town there was always some traffic. Here, there wasn't another car in sight, nor were there any people along this stretch of beach. Just maybe...

"Are you trusting me with your car?" she asked cautiously.

"And why not? Lean close to me and let me explain the mechanics to you." As she did, he went through an explanation of the instruments on the dash, the pedals on the floor and the gearshift lever. "Any questions?"

"I don't know how much good it'll do me to learn to drive your automatic Mustang. Aunt Moira's car is a shift with a clutch that makes her swear."

He had her interested. It was a start. "First things first. Learn to drive this one, then we'll concentrate on the other. Besides, perhaps your father will buy you a brand-new car when he finds out you can drive."

"I would never ask my father—not for a car, not for anything."

Her voice was firm, brooking no argument, Blake noted. "Maybe he'd like to make up for his past behavior."

"He doesn't have to buy me a car to do that. He simply has to...to..." She took in a deep, troubled breath. "I don't want to talk about my father."

"I'm sorry I brought him up. Don't worry about the car. The important thing is that you learn to drive and that you can do on this one. Now watch what I do." Blake slipped out of park, and slowly the car began to move.

Jenny's eyes flickered from his hands to his feet, then out the windshield as he drove past a palm tree, circled it and returned. When he glanced at her expectantly, she nodded. "I'll try it."

Blake changed places with her. "Just relax and you'll do fine."

He needn't have reassured her, he realized soon enough. She handled the whole maneuver flawlessly. Watching her face, he saw that she was delighted with herself, but struggling not to let him see it. He grinned at her. "Piece of cake, right?"

"Not so very difficult," she admitted.

"Let's practice that some more and try a few other things." He had her repeat the same run, then back up along the hard-packed sand, then circle the tree several times. Next he got out and found a stick, then drew lines in the sand.

"I want you to pretend there's a car parked here," he said, pointing the stick to the first position. "And another over here past this line. Now pull up parallel with the first car, then back into this area I've marked off without touching these imaginary cars and still staying within these lines." He tossed aside the stick and dusted off his hands. "Think you can do it?"

"I can try." Foot on the brake, she shifted into reverse, then angled the wheel. But she stepped on the gas with a little too much pressure and she cut across the first line. Skidding across the sand, she braked quickly, jerking to a stop. Sheepishly she looked out the open window at him.

"Well, now you've plowed into the first car and slammed up over the curb. Want to try that again?"

"Don't look so smug, Major. How many times did you have to practice this before you learned it?"

He crossed his arms over his chest. "*I* got it on the first try—with *real* cars in front and back."

Narrowing her eyes, she accepted the challenge. Following the same procedure, she parallel-parked perfectly the second time and sent him a triumphant look. "I suppose it takes two tries for us women," she said sarcastically.

Blake walked over and braced his hands on the window frame. He liked her like this, smiling and pleased with herself. It was so much easier to deal with his feelings for her when he was instructing her in something simple like driving a car. It was when her eyes took on that dark awareness and her scent wrapped itself around him that he lost it.

"Pretty good, lady."

"Thanks." She opened the car door. "Ready to leave?"

He closed the door. "You drive." He walked around and got in on the passenger side.

"Are you sure? I mean, what if we meet another car?"

"He'll go on his way and we'll go on ours. It's only a short distance on a road that's seldom traveled. Besides, I'm right here. Just go easy on the gas pedal, leadfoot." He buckled his seat belt.

Heart in her throat, Jenny set out at a snail's pace. Though her hands were damp, she made it without incident and without running into other traffic. With a sigh of relief she turned into the drive of the cottage and shifted into park. Handing Blake the keys, she let out a nervous laugh. "Now all we have to do is keep the roads clear and I can drive anywhere."

He laughed and got out of the car. The sky was dark for late afternoon, with rolling clouds moving in overhead. "Looks like more rain and soon."

Jenny went inside. "I'll just put your dinner on and be off." Her dog came rushing over to greet her. "Hey, Rafferty, guess who's driving like a pro?" she asked the wiggly pup, leaning down to pet his shaggy head.

"I'll drive you home when you're ready to go," Blake said. "But before you get busy I want to show you something else. You have to learn a few traffic laws in order to pass the test and get a license." He watched her, hoping her confidence level was up enough to accept this.

Immediately Jenny took a step back. "I don't test well. You know that."

Blake took her hand, led her to the couch and handed her a booklet. "I picked this up at the Driver's License Examining Station. It tells you all you need to know. I can read it and drill you on the answers."

"Is the test verbal?"

"No, it's a written test." He let the words hang in the sudden silence.

Jenny felt the room closing in on her, the nervousness that always accompanied any thoughts of written work. "I feel I could learn the mechanics of driving, but this written test..."

"All right, I have another suggestion." He took her hand, wanting the physical contact for added support because he was getting to the hard part. "Dr. Ambrose told me of a woman named Roberta Ames who's a therapist for people with learning disabilities. She's not a doctor. I told her about you and—"

"You went to a stranger and talked about me?"

"Is that so terrible? I want to help you, and this therapist has had very good results. Won't you at least give her a chance?"

Jenny pulled free and stood frozen. "You shouldn't have talked with her until you'd checked with me."

"I didn't give her your name. I only told her your background as it pertains to your reading difficulties. Jenny, did you ever have a serious ear infection?"

Needing to work off her frustration, Jenny began to pace the small room, her hands tightly curled in the pockets of her white slacks. She tried to concentrate on the question at hand. "An ear infection? They tell me I was very sick before leaving Ireland as a baby. Influenza, I believe, but I don't know if it involved the ears. Why?"

"Roberta Ames asked me. Maybe that somehow affected your ability to process information on paper." He got up and went to her, catching her in midstride. "Listen, Jenny, all I'm asking is that you talk with her. I'll go with you."

She was staring at his blue shirt, but she was seeing another time, another place. A brand-new doctor had just finished still another exam, then told her father that he couldn't find anything wrong with Jenny *physically*. The implication had been clear. It had to be in her head. Jenny had jumped out of her chair and started throwing things—books from the shelves, items from the doctor's desktop, anything she could grab.

Lucius had been startled, then furious. He'd tried to catch her, but she'd been too fast for him, rushing all over the room, destroying whatever she could reach. Finally she'd run out of steam and slumped to the floor in a rush of tears. That had been the first of several temper outbursts that had confused and angered her parents.

She had been seven years old with a mother who was slowly dying.

"Jenny, are you listening to me?"

His voice drew her back to the present. "You don't know what you're asking of me, Blake. I can't do it."

Dropping his hands from her, Blake released an exasperated sigh. "You mean you *won't* do it."

"Have it your way."

He felt the anger rising, and this time he didn't fight it. "No, Jenny, it's you who wants it your way. Well, fine. Forget the driving lessons and learning to read. Forget the therapist who wants to help. Stay the way you are. Don't break out of your protective shell. Don't reach your potential. Stay buried in this small town. Grow old here, and bitter, too, as you will sooner or later when you realize that life has passed you by because you were too afraid to try."

Stunned at his outburst, she stared at him. "You don't understand."

"I guess not." Grabbing his cane, Blake turned from her. "I'm going for a walk." As quickly as possible, he left.

She listened to the back door slam, then went to gaze out the kitchen window. He was angrily marching toward the wooded area. The tears rolled down her face, but she barely felt them. Rafferty came bounding over, and she picked him up, cuddling his soft body to hers.

It had been terrible being unable to please her father, worse disappointing her mother and Aunt Moira. But disillusioning Blake was the worst feeling she'd known.

Could she force herself to see the therapist for his sake?

Blake was quite a way into the woods behind his cottage before his anger left him. It happened about the time he jammed his cane into a rabbit hole and heard it snap. "Damn," he muttered out loud.

Served him right, he thought as he stopped to lean against a huge cypress tree heavy with Spanish moss. He had no right to bully Jenny the way he just had. Disgusted with himself, he tossed aside the broken remains of his cane.

All his life he'd hated to see one person browbeat another, and now he'd done it. She was smaller, younger, far more defenseless than he. And she was very inexperienced in standing up for her rights. Though she couldn't read, she was a woman in charge of her own life and should be allowed to make her own decisions. Who had given him the right to boss her around, even if he thought his suggestions were for her own good?

Needing to work off his leftover energy, he began to walk again, only more slowly this time, threading his way through the thick foliage. Just recently he had turned away from the doctors who'd given him suggestions "for his own good." Now he'd fallen into the same shoddy practice—telling Jenny what was *good* for her. People trying to run other people's lives, Blake thought with self-derision. Wrong, all of it was wrong.

Jenny had lived a difficult life so far, losing her mother at such a young age, considered dumb by a father who'd later turned his back on her, thrust aside by a self-centered stepmother. Thank goodness her aunt had seen the beauty inside Jenny. Still, Jenny had lived on the fringes of life, absorbing knowledge where and when she could. Surprisingly she'd emerged a wonderful, intelligent, giving person. And this was the woman he'd attacked.

As he strolled along berating himself, Blake felt the first of the rain falling through the leaves. Glancing up, he saw that the sky had grown quite dark. The storm he'd predicted earlier was here, just when his anger had taken him deep into the woods.

Listening to a rumble of thunder, Blake tried to ascertain whether it would be a short squall or continue well into the evening. It wasn't falling too heavily yet, so he started back.

He would make it up to Jenny, he thought as he retraced his steps. He would ask her to forgive his meddling and assure her that he'd stop nagging. The tenuous friendship they'd developed—the only one of any consequence he'd managed since arriving in Florida—was important to him.

He cared about her, Blake finally admitted to himself, much more than he had planned. He still didn't want long-term involvement, but friendship was another matter. She was a woman who seemed able to look past his physical imperfections and see the man inside. That alone was worth protecting.

The rain had drenched his shirt and pants and his shoes were soggy underfoot. He was also getting tired. There were areas of wild grass slippery from the rain, making walking more difficult. Spotting a good size tree, he decided he'd stop and wait out the worst of the storm. He ducked under, sat down on a gnarled piece of trunk sticking out of the ground and leaned back under the protection of the overhanging leaves.

Watching a flash of lightning skitter through the trees, he hoped Jenny had the good sense not to start for home in a downpour.

Jenny shoved the meat loaf into the oven and closed the door. A sudden lightning bolt split the sky, drawing her attention to the kitchen window. When had it grown so dark? she wondered, wiping her hands. She'd been so preoccupied with her thoughts and with hurrying to put together dinner so she could leave that she hadn't even noticed the rain beginning. Now she could see that it was coming down in heavy sheets, the sky dark with murky gray clouds overhead.

She checked her watch and saw it wasn't yet five. When had Blake marched off? Over an hour ago. He should have been back by now. Squinting through the window, she wondered where he was. Nervously Jenny unbraided her hair, running her fingers through its length as she watched the falling rain.

Growing more concerned by the minute, she went out onto the porch. Rafferty bounded out with her, sniffed the air, then wandered out into the grass. In the distance she could see the ocean waves rising high as they hit the sandy shoreline, the sea and the sky merging in a swirl of gray. Not a soul could be seen. She gazed toward the back woods and saw only the rain shrouding the trees. Was Blake in there or had he come out and walked toward the beach? Despite the storm, the air was warm, causing misty vapors to rise. Thunder boomed again, the only sound other than the splash of rain from the roof onto the walkway.

There wasn't a sign of Blake anywhere.

As her eyes searched the area, she saw Rafferty disappear into the trees. Silly dog, wanting to be out in all this. Jenny went back inside, her heart pounding.

Why had she been so stubborn? Why hadn't she given in to Blake's request? What was one more therapist after all the doctors she'd seen? If she'd agreed, he wouldn't have left in anger and he wouldn't be out there now, perhaps hurt, perhaps bleeding. When he returned, she'd let him take her to his therapist. Anything to have Blake safe again, with her again.

The thunder sounded overhead, louder than before, and Jenny cringed. Scarcely aware of the tears that ran down her cheeks like the rivulets of rain on the window, she began to pray.

It was lasting too long, Blake thought, and turning into a full-fledged electrical storm. He'd been foolish to think he could wait it out. Pushing to his feet, he stood.

Again he started back, hoping he was on the right path. In the deepening shadows, the zigzagging growth of trees was confusing. Parting the branches with his hands, he walked carefully, realizing that a fall now would be his undoing.

For what seemed like long minutes he trudged on. Thunder was sounding more frequently now, as if in rolling waves. Perhaps that meant the storm was moving on out to sea. Blake hoped so as he took a moment to wipe away the moisture on his face. Standing still, he thought he heard a sound. He cocked his head, listening. But he heard only the wind whining through the trees.

Suddenly, above the sound of the storm, he heard two sharp barks. Could Rafferty have wandered out into the woods? He called out the dog's name, then waited. He barely had time to brace himself when the ball of gray fur hurled itself at him. "Hey, boy. What are you doing out here?"

But the dog didn't want to lick his face this time, or take the time to play. He wiggled out of Blake's grasp and began running down the path leading out of the woods, stopping every few feet to look back, as if checking to see that Blake was following.

Carefully following Rafferty, Blake kept up a steady pace. He walked slowly so as not to slip on the wet grass. His knee ached, but no more than usual. Finally, after what seemed like a long while, he could see the light from the cabin's kitchen window glowing through the trees. Keeping his eyes on it, he plodded along.

At last Rafferty ran out of the woods and into the yard, followed moments later by Blake. Just a few more yards and he'd be there, he thought as the rain pelted his head and ran down his back.

Hearing a noise on the porch, Jenny rushed to the back door. Rafferty stood there dripping wet, his hind end wagging. And coming toward them was Blake, muddy and soaked, his hair plastered to his head. Never had he looked so wonderful. She hurried out onto the porch as he hauled himself up the steps.

Jenny rushed at him, her arms winding around him, her voice a sob that got buried in his neck as she pulled him closer. Tears streamed from under her closed lids as she clung to him, overcome with emotion.

"I'm sorry, Jenny," he said, his mouth close to her ear.

"It's all right," she said, the words barely audible, caught in a hiccup.

"No, it isn't." He'd been foolish to march off angry, crazy to leave her, Blake realized at that moment as he drew back and looked into her anxious eyes. "It was wrong of me. I shouldn't have left like that. I'm sorry I worried you."

Jenny's lips trembled. "I thought I'd lost you, that I'd made you so angry you'd rushed off and gotten hurt because of me."

For Blake then the storm disappeared and the pain in his leg was forgotten. The world slipped away and there was only this woman and the way she made him feel. As her arms drew him nearer, he closed his eyes and kissed her deeply. She opened to him avidly, as eager as he.

A noise was roaring in his ears as he kissed her lips, her face, her closed eyelids. The overwhelming rush of feeling was contagious. Jenny rained kisses on his temple, the corners of his mouth and where his pulse pounded in his throat. Blake's heart hammered and his blood churned as he pulled back again to look at her. He couldn't find the words to tell her all he felt, so he just stared into her lovely face, hoping she could see what he couldn't seem to say.

At last Jenny smiled—unrestrained, undoubting. His eyes had revealed all she needed to know. "I don't want to be just your friend anymore, Blake," she said very softly. "I want to be your lover."

Chapter Eight

He lit candles, a chunky one in a brass holder and a tall, tapered one of pale blue, and placed them on the oak dresser. The pungent aroma of vanilla drifted to Jenny as she took the thick yellow towel Blake handed her. The light flickered over his bare chest as he rubbed rainwater from his hair, then draped the blue towel around his neck. Sitting in the middle of his bed and drying off, she watched him as her heartbeat escalated.

Outside, the rain beat against the roof and pounded on the windows of the small cottage. The wind whirled, bending the palm trees and causing them to brush against the sides of the house. Occasional flashes of lightning streaked eerily through the evening sky, followed by claps of thunder that rolled in from the sea. Jenny neither saw nor heard any of it.

She saw only the dark gray depths of Blake's eyes as he handed her a snifter of brandy, and she heard only the thrumming of her own pulse as she waited for his reaction to the boldest statement she'd ever made in her life.

Silently he sat down on the bed alongside her, his expression unreadable. She'd had little experience in flirtation, none in seduction. But he'd been silent so long that she had to say something. Deciding it would be more strategic to retreat than advance, she offered him a way out. "Of course, if you don't want me as a lover..."

"I think you know better than that."

Jenny took a small swallow of the brandy, hoping he'd think it was for heat rather than courage, then set the glass on the nightstand. "I'm not very good at this."

Blake eased her back onto the pillow, leaning down until he was very close. "Just one question, Jenny. Are you sure? Because I can't give you the words you might need, the commitment you might want."

She'd known that and, though the disappointment was there, she would deal with it later. She'd known from the beginning that one day he would leave. But tonight—and perhaps for a while yet—she would have him. She couldn't let him go without knowing what it would be like to let him love her.

"I'm not asking for forever, just for tonight." Her voice was low, husky. "We may not be right for each other, but I can't seem to stop wanting you."

"And I can't get you off my mind." He couldn't give her promises, but he could give her the gift of his feelings, something he rarely shared. Slowly he ran his fingers up into her hair. "I wake each morning and you're my first thought. Even before acknowledging the discomfort of an aching body, I think of you. And somehow the pain isn't as bad.''

He felt her hands flutter to his chest and settle there. ''At night as I lie down your face is the one I close my eyes on. I hear your laughter, I smell your fragrance, I see your eyes as they study me. And I fall asleep with thoughts of you.''

In the candlelight his eyes were smoky with the beginning of desire. She would believe him now, Jenny decided, if only because she badly wanted to. ''I'm so afraid I won't please you.''

''That's not possible.'' It was the way he'd dreamed it would be, the way he'd been afraid to imagine it could be. The wind and the rain pummeled the little cottage, but they were safe and warm inside, sheltered from the elements and from a world neither of them was comfortable with. Here, they were alone, alone in their own special space. ''I've wanted you for so long,'' he said, his fingers tangling in her thick hair.

Jenny saw a quick flicker of nerves pass over his features, and it quieted her own. He, too, was a little hesitant; the thought relieved her. She would have truly felt inadequate if he had been supremely confident. Excitement rose in her, dizzying in its intensity. Silently she pulled the towel from him and moved her hands to encircle his neck, urging him nearer.

Blake's lips touched hers, gently at first, then gradually increasing the pressure. Did she taste sweeter than yesterday because of the realizations he'd come to in the woods? Blake wondered as he took her deeper. Did her arms hold him tighter, her touch excite him more because suddenly he was free to linger and savor? Did her scent intoxicate him more tonight because she was reaching for him eagerly, or was he just heady from the feel of her? He didn't know. He only knew that loving had never been this sweet before.

Jenny closed her eyes on a sigh as his mouth moved down to explore her throat, then trailed upward again to kiss the spot behind her ear. Inside she felt a liquid warmth spreading and knew it had nothing to do with the brandy she'd tasted. Nothing had ever set her on fire the way Blake's hands did as they eased her damp clothes off, dropping them to the floor.

Her own hands wandered up his bare back; her loving fingers soothed the tiny scars they encountered. The joy of being free to touch him as she had longed to made her more daring. She caressed the curly hair of his chest, reveling in the strong muscles beneath. Drunk with desire, she let her fingers trail down to his flat stomach and felt his skin quiver at the contact.

Jenny had thought she'd be embarrassed, at the least shy, under his heated gaze. But instead she felt only the delight she saw reflected in his dark eyes as they roamed over her. Involuntarily she arched toward him and his fingers moved to stroke her aching breasts. In moments his mouth followed his hands, and she was steeped in mind-shattering pleasure.

How did he know where she wanted him to touch— the spot she craved to be kissed, the place where no man's lips had ever lingered? She inhaled his rich male scent, then shifted to taste the rain-splattered flavor of his skin. His hands closed over hers then, and he moved her arms above her head. Carefully he lowered to rub his chest over her swollen breasts, and Jenny heard herself moan out loud.

Blake slanted his mouth over hers, swallowing the sweet sounds she made as she moved beneath him, driving them both closer to the madness. Her lips were hungry on his now as her needs intensified, her small hands gripping his fingers, her heart pounding against his. She'd come alive, throbbing with an edgy passion she'd never dreamed herself capable of.

His lips kept her distracted while he slid one hand down her sleek body. When his fingers touched where no man had dared, she jolted in his arms, then quieted as he whispered softly in her ear. The more he touched, the more he wanted. Lost in her, he returned to kiss her mouth, his tongue taking possession of hers.

Control was something Blake seldom had trouble with, but he was fighting for it now. She was more responsive than he'd hoped, her rising passion matching his. Pulling back, he caught his breath as he stared into the dark beauty of her eyes.

Heart pounding, chest heaving, Jenny moved one hand to the snap of his jeans, impatience making her brave.

He smiled then, but moved her hand aside and pulled off the rest of his clothes. Grabbing the comforter from the foot of the bed, he settled it over them before turning to her.

Jenny went still, knowing how he felt about exposing his scars to her. But she had revealed everything to him and would accept no less in return. "No more hiding, Blake," she said softly. "Not from me." With a quick thrust she tossed the comforter from the bed.

His eyes smoldered for a long moment, then he let out a deep breath. "I'm continually amazed at the things you can get me to do." He kissed the corners of her mouth. "Maybe it's because you're so very beautiful."

Even if he was exaggerating, tonight she would believe him, Jenny thought. His hands were moving on her again, and her excitement mounted. "I want to touch you," she whispered into his ear.

He hesitated briefly, then moved her hand between their bodies. He watched her lovely face as she learned him, then closed his eyes on a groan of pleasure he couldn't prevent. Knowing he couldn't hold out much longer, he shifted, his mouth capturing hers.

She returned his kiss, and in no time he had her breathless again. Then he was filling her and, though she'd both longed for and feared the moment, she felt only joy. He moved slowly within her, then more rapidly. Jenny could only cling to him, her heart racing. Climbing, climbing, she let him take her.

Blake watched her cheeks grow rosy and damp. He'd made love before, or thought he had. But it had been nothing like this. Never had he needed like this, been overwhelmed like this, wanted to please another like this. The storm blustered away outside, but inside he was aware of only Jenny, her eyes closing now. Jenny, with her giving nature, tangling his emotions. Jenny, whose body offered him solace and peace.

He felt her arch once more as her hands on his back dug into his flesh. Then they were both sailing together in an endless blue sky.

She lay snuggled beneath him for long minutes. Or was it hours? Time had lost meaning for Jenny. His heart beat against hers and her legs were twined with his along with the tangled sheet. Through a bright haze of feeling she felt stunned.

No one had ever tried to describe this to her; no one could have. The dramas she'd seen hadn't even come close to the reality. She had lived in her body every day of her life and never known what it was capable of. With a certainty born in her woman's heart she knew she'd never be the same again.

Innocence wasn't a thing she'd particularly prided herself on. Nor, except for a few early dire warnings, was it a subject of many discussions in her aunt's house. She supposed, by today's standards, she'd been slow in offering herself to someone. The truth was, though she'd experienced curiosity, she'd never known need until Blake had come into her life.

Blake's breathing leveled off slowly as his mind began to clear. His face was buried in her neck and her arms were wrapped around him. Still buried deep inside her, he could feel the lingering remnants of passion pulsating. Thinking his weight must be crushing her, he started to draw back, but her small hands tightened at his back.

"Don't leave me, not yet," she murmured.

He lifted his head and saw that her face was rosy and her eyes heavy-lidded. He thought she was the most beautiful woman he'd ever seen. He placed a gentle kiss on the tip of her nose. "You won't be able to move if I don't get up soon."

"I don't want to move ever again." A sigh trembled from between her swollen lips.

Feeling content, he snuggled down again, inhaling the well-loved flavor of her skin. He felt her shudder and raised a hand to stroke her cheek. "What was that?"

"My aunt says that when you shiver like that someone's just walked over your grave. Silly, I suppose."

"Not so silly." Rolling onto his back, Blake took her with him and cradled her against his chest. "I was almost in a fiery grave, but for some reason I'm still here. Since then I've realized that planning for the future can be disastrous. Tomorrow is for fools. I once had my whole life mapped out right down to the woman to take for a wife—not because I loved her but because she would fit in—and the 2.3 children we would have, the national norm. I would fly and I would teach, and we would live the good life. Then, in the space of a few minutes, everything changed."

There was a message there for her, Jenny was certain. He was telling her that, though making love was fine, she shouldn't make too much of their being together. She pushed back the hurt as she inched back from him. She would ease his mind. She also had a small vestige of pride to protect. "I think you're right. I've never been big on planning ahead. One day at a time seems safer."

Glad that she felt the same way, Blake lay listening again to the rain. A sudden tug of conscience had him frowning. "I should get you home. Moira will be worried."

Minutes ago they'd been wrapped together in passion. Now he wanted her gone, Jenny realized. If she hadn't known what loving him would be like, she hadn't even come close to guessing what the aftermath would be like. Feeling suddenly chilled, she moved off the bed and searched for her discarded clothes.

He didn't want her to leave, but how could he ask her to stay? Blake thought. There was her reputation in this small town to consider, and her aunt's censure to look forward to if she spent the night with him. "The storm seems to have let up," Blake said, rising also and going to the closet for dry jeans. A sudden burst of thunder underscored the lie.

"Yes." She turned so he wouldn't see the tears that had sprung to her eyes. "I'll need to borrow something. My clothes are still wet."

"I'll get you a shirt." He rummaged through his closet, his heart heavy. She seemed suddenly anxious to rush off. Perhaps, with the heat of passion cooling, the sight of his scarred body had turned her off. He should be pleased she wasn't clinging to him, Blake told himself as he grabbed a shirt and turned to her.

She took it without looking at him and shrugged into it. He stood watching the back of her bent head as she fumbled with the buttons. She looked so small, so fragile. He badly wanted to touch her, but he hesitated. Confidence hadn't been a steady companion of late. It wasn't until he saw her shoulders shaking slightly that he decided to hell with what anyone else thought. "Don't go," he said into the quiet room.

Jenny stopped, unsure of what she'd heard. Swiveling slowly, she looked up at him, unaware of the tears trailing down her cheeks.

A myriad of emotions warred inside him. He shouldn't ask her to stay yet, God help him, that was what he desperately wanted. "Don't go, Jenny," Blake said, more firmly this time. "Please stay with me."

With a ragged sigh she rushed into his arms, her mouth finding his. Over and over she kissed his lips, his face, her tears dampening both of them. "I didn't think you wanted me with you."

"I *do,* though. It's not the best thing for either of us probably, but I want you with me." He drew back to look into her eyes. "What about your aunt? She's already questioned my feelings for you. She wouldn't approve of your staying with me."

"I live in her house, but she doesn't rule me. Not in this, never in this. No one should tell a grown woman who to want or what to do."

He held her loosely, stroking the smooth skin of her back beneath his shirt. "I worry she won't understand, a woman who's never married."

"Ah, but you don't have to be married to know what it is to want a man. There was someone in Moira's life once. He was twenty and she only seventeen. But he chose another and she no longer speaks of him, though I know she's not forgotten. We Ryans tend to be fiercely protective about our feelings."

His hands trailed down her back and he lifted her slightly, pressing himself closer to her heat. Her response was instantaneous and avid as she returned the pressure. Her sensuality had lain dormant but, once awakened, was as natural to her as breathing. "You Ryans tend to be fierce about many things."

She cocked her head. "You noticed, did you?" Her hands slid up his chest, then stopped. Her fingertips found a jagged scar, then a faint indentation of puckered skin. In the candlelight she saw what she hadn't noticed in the bed. Myriad marks of the suffering he'd endured. She raised pain-filled eyes to his. "How did you ever live through all that horror?"

He stiffened. "I don't want your pity, Jenny."

"That isn't even close to what I feel." She touched her lips to one scar, then another and still more. Long minutes later, when she rose on tiptoe to touch her mouth to his, she heard his sigh of welcome.

It wasn't pity he tasted in her kiss; it was passion. He'd meant to tease for a while, to stoke her desires to full readiness. But her mouth was suddenly demanding as she shifted to nip at his ears, to taste his neck, her tongue arousing him, weakening him. She wanted no slow loving this time, he decided as he shoved off his jeans. He would see to it that she got what she wanted.

The wind buffeted the windows as he showered kisses over her skin, feeling her grow hot and damp under his restless mouth. He sought out every weak and vulnerable spot he could reach with his clever tongue, his seeking hands, until he saw she was burning for him as he burned for her. He heard her murmur his name and grew bolder, his lips journeying down past her flat stomach.

Unbearable excitement skittered along Jenny's nerve endings. He'd taught her to want and, oh, how she wanted. She felt fiercely alive, wonderfully free, capable of anything. When his mouth settled on her, she heard her own hoarse cry and felt her heart thudding wildly. As she peaked, her breath came in short, ragged puffs. Boneless, she went limp in his arms.

But he was far from finished with her. His blood pounding, Blake skimmed back up to swallow her moans and capture her mouth with his. Her body was a furnace, hot and waiting, as he lay full-length over her.

Sanity shattered as he made her his, desperate with need for her as passion hammered through him. Her hips arched to meet his thrusts, her breath harsh in his ears, as he drove them both to the point of delirium. Together they raced to a shattering finish.

The bedside phone woke them. From years of training Blake was instantly alert. Jenny came awake more slowly, shoving her hair back from a sleepy face. Blake answered on the second ring.

He listened quietly for a moment. "Yes, she is. Just a moment." He covered the mouthpiece. "It's Moira."

She glanced at the clock and nearly groaned aloud. Eight and still raining, she saw through the window. Not only raining but already dark. Of course, her aunt would be worried. Jenny wasn't usually so inconsiderate. She took the phone and tried for an even tone. "I should have called you sooner, Aunt Moira. I'm sorry if I worried you."

"It's no problem as long as you're all right. I just made it home from the library and found you hadn't been here since morning. And the storm..." Concern thickened the older woman's brogue.

"Yes, Blake was out in it and—"

"Out in such weather! What on earth would he be doing that for?"

"It wasn't raining when he left the house and... Not to worry. He's safe and dry now." Jenny sat up, an unfamiliar guilt making her hand tremble as she pulled the sheet up to cover her breasts.

She glanced at Blake lying back and quietly watching her. Their time together hadn't been nearly long enough. She found she wanted badly to sleep with him until morning. "Since it's still coming down, I'd thought I might just stay here the night." She closed her eyes, picturing the shock that must be spreading over her aunt's face.

It took Moira a moment to recover. "Did you now? Tell me, lass, are you saying what I think you are?"

Jenny lifted her chin just a fraction. She wouldn't feel shame, not for what she and Blake had shared. "Yes."

"I see." The pause was longer this time. "Do you love him, Jenny?"

She shifted her eyes to Blake's face, knowing he couldn't hear the question. "Yes, Aunt Moira." She said it with pride, not defiance. Unable to stop herself, she reached to lace her fingers with his.

"Then there's not much more for me to be saying, is there?" Moira asked. "Except perhaps to be careful, lass. I hope I've taught you to think of more than just the moment."

"You've taught me a great deal and I remember it all. Please don't worry."

"I'll try not to. One last thing. Keep in mind that some hearts mend more slowly than others, and some not at all. Do you understand, lass?"

"Yes." Now it was Jenny who took a moment. "Please don't be disappointed in me." She wished she didn't feel the need for her aunt's approval, but she did.

"Disappointed in you? Never. I well remember a woman's needs, and I knew this was but a matter of days away the last time we spoke of the captain. Your love for him was in your eyes."

She hadn't known that. "Thank you."

"I just don't want to see you hurt."

"I don't want that, either. I love you."

"And I, you. Good night, lass."

Slowly Jenny hung up the phone and let out a breathy sigh.

"Everything all right?" Blake asked, having tried to guess the other side of the conversation.

She nodded as Blake pulled her down to him and waited until she folded her arms over his chest. Her expression was thoughtful, but her slightly swollen mouth was evidence of a long evening of loving. He liked seeing her like this—soft and sleepy-eyed, with that just-loved look on her face. "Regrets?"

"About being here with you? No, none."

"Then what is it that makes you suddenly sad?"

"I've been thinking. Blake, I'll go see your therapist, if you still want me to. I don't want you, or anyone else, to be ashamed of me."

His hand had pushed into her hair so quickly that she scarcely noticed. Gripping a handful, he narrowed his eyes at her and pulled her closer. "Don't you *ever* downgrade yourself to me, or to anyone else. You are so much more than most educated people I've known. And . . ."

"And I could be more. I know. So make the appointment."

He didn't bother to hide his surprised pleasure. "Are you sure? I don't want you to do this for me."

"I promised myself, as I waited for you to return, that if you came back safely, I'd do what you asked."

He shook his head. "No, I want you to *want* to go. No bargaining with God, or me."

"I'm not, truly. I should have gone in the first place. I was afraid. I *am* afraid. But I'll go, providing you'll go with me." Because now she had a greater need. If there ever was to be a future for her and Blake—and she couldn't stop wishing there could be one day—she'd have to be more than she had been so far. There was his family to consider. What would they think if they came here and met her, a small-town woman who couldn't read or write? The thought made her shudder. "Yes, I want to go."

"Good, because I think you have great potential, Jenny Starbuck." His fingers trailed down the silk of her cheek.

"Perhaps it was destiny that sent you to me."

"Perhaps destiny sent me here to push you into seeking help about reading."

She smiled into his eyes. "Or maybe the fates sent me to you, Major Hanley, to see to your house and...a few of your other needs."

"And here I didn't think you believed in such nonsense."

Her hand moved to touch his face, loving the freedom to do so. "Me, not believe? I'm the Irish one here, the one who was brought up on stories of mystical beings like fairies and leprechauns. Oh, I believe, all right."

"I believe in something, too."

"What's that?"

"I believe my stomach thinks my throat's been cut. Since you're spending the night—with your aunt's permission—I wonder if we could take time out to eat a bite or so?"

"Men!" Jenny said with mock disdain. "All you ever think of is your empty bellies."

His hand slid down along the smooth line of her back suggestively. "It's not *all* we think of."

Chapter Nine

Roberta Ames didn't really have an office as such. As a learning disability instructor and speech therapist, she served several small communities on Florida's eastern coast from Fort Lauderdale at the northern end to Hialeah in the south. Mostly she would meet with students during school in classrooms specially set up for that purpose by the Special Education Department. However, adults who sought her services were invited to her small condominium in Apaloosa, where a second bedroom had been converted into a home office.

Pulling up in front of the address she'd given him on the phone, Blake shut off the engine and turned to Jenny beside him. She'd been alternately chattering nervously, then quietly subdued on the way over. Now she glanced at Roberta's front door with obvious reluctance. "Do you want me to wait in the car?" he asked gently.

Jenny set aside the tissue she'd been shredding in her damp hands and shook her head. "You can come in if you want." She wanted him with her, yet the thought of it unnerved her. She hated having Blake see firsthand how frustrated she became when faced with questions and testing. But if he did, he might realize the futility of his search for an answer to her problem and back off.

Or Roberta Ames would pull off a miracle and the gods would smile on her for a change. Jenny stepped out of the car.

Blake pushed the doorbell and gave her hand a squeeze. He found her fingers cool despite the heat of midday.

In moments Roberta smiled a welcome through the screen door and stood aside to let them in. Appearing to be in her mid-forties, she had short black hair and warm brown eyes and wore huge hoop earrings with a businesslike silk blouse and skirt. Her small living room was comfortably cluttered and noticeably chilly, Blake thought as he looked around.

"I hope you don't mind air-conditioning," Roberta said as she patted her damp brow with a white handkerchief. "These damn hot flashes are driving me crazy." Her eyes briefly flickered to Blake's bandaged cheek, then met his direct gaze.

"It's a welcome change," Blake assured her. Jenny's hand in his gripped harder. Before she could bolt and run he introduced her to the therapist.

Roberta's smile returned. "I'm glad you could make it, Jenny. Why don't you have a seat in here, Blake,

while Jenny and I go into my office? Right this way.''
She turned down a short hallway.

Jenny let go of his hand and, wearing a worried
frown, followed Roberta Ames. Blake heard the door
close and sat down.

There were magazines on a low coffee table. He
picked one up after another, idly flipping through
several. He didn't want to read about the country's
budget deficit, nor about how best to can peaches.
Restlessly he stood and walked to stand at the picture
window, his hands in his pockets.

Jenny was frightened, he knew, and his thoughts
were in there with her. If only Roberta Ames's training held the answer to Jenny's problem. Not for his
sake, but for Jenny's. He knew her reluctance was
rooted in past frustrations at the vain attempts of
doctors to analyze her situation, not in lack of desire
to find an answer. She'd confided some of the details
of those childhood visits to him last night.

Last night. Involuntarily he smiled. They'd managed to salvage the overdone meat loaf and had shared
a late dinner. Wearing only his shirt, which trailed
down to her knees, Jenny had insisted they eat by
candlelight. Blake had poured each of them some
wine, but they'd barely tasted it. They'd been drunk
on each other, frequently reaching to touch a hand to
a cheek, stopping for a lingering kiss, spending an in-
ordinate amount of time just gazing into each other's
eyes.

The rain hadn't let up all night, but they hadn't
minded. The sound against the windows made the inside seem more cozy and private. They had stacked the
dishes in the sink and returned to his bedroom, and to
the newly discovered wonder they'd found in the big

four-poster bed. They had made love, then held each other and talked, then made love again. Layer upon layer of pleasure had built until at last they'd fallen asleep holding hands. Blake had never known that such intimacy was possible between two people.

Pillow talk, something else he'd not experienced before. His past relationships with other women, including Eleanor, had never entailed long, leisurely conversations after the loving. The fault had been his, not theirs. Never before had he felt the need to know someone so thoroughly, or to speak of his own feelings so openly. Not until Jenny.

She'd asked about the details of his accident and, for the first time, he'd found himself sharing his feelings about those terrible months. She had listened quietly, then he'd looked over and seen that her face was wet from the tears she'd shed for his pain. Later he had asked about her family, and she'd spoken of her father and Jocelyn and what she remembered of the turbulent few years after her mother's death. She talked of how she'd struggled not to feel dumb when so many had insisted she was. He had wanted so badly to erase those awful memories. He wanted to prove to the world how wonderful she was.

She *was* wonderful, but the feelings between them couldn't last. It was just that he needed someone now while he was recovering—someone who hadn't known him before and wouldn't be comparing his former self with the man he'd become. And Jenny needed someone to push her into finding help with her reading problem. Two people in need who had met at the right time, that was what they were. They would touch each other's life for a short time, then move on with fond memories.

Turning, Blake gazed down the hallway toward the closed door, wondering why the scenario he pictured didn't sit too well with him.

"Now just take your time, Jenny, and tell me how you see the letters on this page." Roberta held the book open on the desk.

Seated next to her, Jenny recited the letters she saw. This was different than anything she'd been asked to do before. Always before doctors had just instructed her to read the lines, and when she was unable to the session had usually ended. Roberta had first given her a long verbal quiz and then had turned to books.

"Fine." Roberta made a notation on a yellow pad and turned the page of the book. "You've told me you know your numbers. Read these for me, please."

The first group was easy, but she found the second series more confusing. "I think that's fifteen, then sixty-one. On this line, that's forty-four and this is fifty-four." Jenny leaned back as Roberta jotted more notes. This was the third book they'd gone through, and still the instructor hadn't given her a clue as to how she was doing.

Roberta tapped her pen against the pad and looked at Jenny thoughtfully. "A few general questions now, if you don't mind. You mentioned that you'd had influenza as a baby. Did the illness include an ear infection?"

"I've checked with my aunt and she only remembers that I was very sick for about two weeks, but it's been over twenty years ago and she doesn't remember specifics."

"Do you recall sleepwalking as a child, or perhaps bedwetting?"

"I don't remember sleepwalking, but I did wet the bed."

"For how long?"

"Until I was nine or ten, until after I'd left my father's house."

"And until after you were taken out of school and no longer being tested, is that right?" As Jenny nodded, Roberta wrote. "Do you recall stuttering back then?"

"Occasionally. My father would keep at me and I couldn't get the answers out quickly enough. I remember having a lot of stomachaches."

"And they, too, disappeared when you left him?"

"Yes, shortly after."

"I see. Did any of the doctors who examined you ever prescribe medication for your problem?"

"One wanted to put me on tranquilizers. I used to have these temper outbursts. But my mother wouldn't allow it."

Roberta nodded and checked off something on her sheet. "Do you take any vitamins currently?"

"No. I'm fairly healthy and I've not thought a supplement necessary."

"When was your last physical and who is your doctor?"

"About a year ago, just a general exam with Dr. Chet Ambrose."

"Would you object if I talked with him about your medical records?"

"Not if it will help." Growing anxious, Jenny leaned forward. "What are you getting at, Miss Ames?"

"Please call me Roberta. I've got something in mind, but just a few more questions first. Quickly raise your right hand."

Jenny's eyes automatically went to her watch on her left wrist, then she raised her other arm.

Roberta nodded. "Do you recall having trouble tying your shoelaces as a child?"

Despite the chilly room, Jenny felt her face heating. "It still takes me a while to tie something. It's so frustrating. I can manage buttons quite well now, but when I was younger they stymied me, too."

Roberta's smile was filled with warmth and understanding. "One last question. What time is it?"

Nervously Jenny looked at her watch and told her.

"Good." The therapist put down her notes. "This is a personal question, Jenny. Mr. Hanley called me about you and—"

"It's *Major* Hanley. He's on medical leave from the air force."

"Oh, I see. At any rate, I don't know what your relationship is with him, but he seemed genuinely concerned about you. Do you want me to share my findings with both of you, or do you want me to talk with you privately?"

Jenny felt a flutter of fear in her stomach as well as a hesitant disbelief. "Forgive me, Roberta, if I seem skeptical, but are you saying that you know what my problem is after asking me questions for an hour when half a dozen doctors and constant testing never uncovered a thing?"

"I understand your hesitancy, but the disorder I believe you have was largely misdiagnosed back when you were a child. Actually, it still often is, and misunderstood, as well, though it affects approximately twenty percent of the world's population."

"What is it?"

"It's a scrambling disorder known as dyslexia. Have you heard of it?"

"No." Jenny found her hands were trembling. "Is it curable?"

"Not curable, but there is help. I need to talk with Dr. Ambrose about a treatment I recommend. Some wonderful inroads have been made using a combination of vitamins, especially B complex, together with antihistamines and niacin. There's some evidence that people who suffer from dyslexia have a balance problem related to inner-ear dysfunction. They have a deficiency, and with the proper medical program the body learns to compensate."

"You mean all I have to do is take a few vitamins and I'll be able to learn to read?"

Roberta smiled as she shook her head. "It's not quite that simple. However, it isn't terribly complicated, either. In conjunction with your doctor we'd start you on the vitamin therapy. Then when your system begins to absorb the medication, you and I would meet and begin reading instructions. You can train yourself to reverse the letters and unscramble words."

"You've known this to work on others?"

"Absolutely. Some can be weaned off the medication eventually, but others have to be on it always. I worked with a young boy of twelve just last year. He'd forget to take his medicine some mornings and all the symptoms would return. He'd take the pills, and in a little over half an hour he was calm and could read again."

"I'm stunned, truly. I came because...well, because Blake was so insistent. But I must admit I didn't hold out much hope. This is fantastic." Smiling, she rose. "I'd like Blake to hear your diagnosis."

"Of course. Let's go to the living room."

With Jenny at his side trying to contain her excitement, Blake listened to Roberta Ames explain her findings.

"Dyslexia is sometimes referred to as mirror vision because its victims see words backward. For instance, *was* would be viewed as *saw*. The problem with all too many testers in the past is that they were interested in numbers and scores only. Dyslexic children usually score very high on IQ tests for their age, provided they're properly tested and verbally questioned."

"And the dysfunction is related somehow to the inner ear?" Blake asked.

Roberta nodded in agreement. "It's thought so, yes. In some victims it's intensified by an early infection. In others, they're born that way. Dyslexia can be inherited, though it isn't always. The unfortunate part is that many dyslexics are misdiagnosed as mentally retarded."

Jenny squeezed Blake's hand. "Perhaps my aunt in Ireland is also dyslexic and not retarded."

"There are often more than one in a family," Roberta went on. "You have several of the classic symptoms. You see numbers and letters scrambled or reversed. For instance, in a sequence you read to me forty-four, then fifty-four, when in fact the second number was forty-five. You also have directional confusion. Do you always wear your watch on your left wrist?"

Jenny smiled. "It's the only way I can tell my left from my right."

"A common problem with dyslexics and one that's not likely to go away. You're also gifted musically, I understand, a compensatory talent that often accompanies the disorder. The temper tantrums were likely a child's answer to frustration. The bedwetting, the stuttering, the school phobia—all symptoms. When you moved to live with your aunt, away from the pressure of your father demanding constant testing, some of the anxiety symptoms disappeared. You learned to adjust, as most of us do."

"Perhaps, but I never stopped wanting to read. To be labeled unteachable is so demoralizing."

Roberta's eyes were soft with understanding. "Of course, it is. But you're *not* unteachable. As a matter of fact, once you begin the program, you'll be amazed how quickly you'll learn."

Jenny could hardly sit still. "When can we begin?"

Smiling, Roberta stood, again mopping her damp cheeks. "Let me discuss my findings with Dr. Ambrose and set up an appointment for you with him. Then let's wait a week after you start your vitamin therapy and then have you come back here. I'll have the books that we'll need to start with by that time."

Blake rose to shake her hand. "I can't thank you enough."

Jenny had a fleeting moment of doubt. "You're sure now? You're not just guessing . . ."

"I'm sure," Roberta said. "I'll prove it all to you by next week."

Impulsively Jenny hugged the older woman before rushing out the door. Pulling Blake's arm to her side, she beamed. "Can you believe it? Can you *honestly* believe I'll soon be able to read? And to write?"

Stopping at the car, he turned to take her into his arms for a quiet moment. "I've believed it all along."

She let out a relieved sigh. "You can't know what it's like to have everyone regard you as dull-witted or stupid."

"It's wonderful seeing you like this, Jenny." Wonderful and slightly scary, Blake thought as he held her close.

Had he just set into motion the very action that would take Jenny from him? But how could he not have opened that door for her?

Wanting to share her happiness, Blake put on a smile and helped Jenny into the car.

The next few weeks whizzed by for Jenny. In conjunction with Roberta Ames Dr. Ambrose started her on her vitamin therapy medication, and soon after she began spending two hours a morning with the instructor, learning to read. Aunt Moira, thrilled at the prospect of Jenny's education beginning, had rearranged her hours at the library in order to drive her.

Afternoons, Jenny would work at Blake's cottage. Then, after dinner, he'd listen while she practiced reading out loud to him. Everyone was pleased with her rapid progress and delighted that her disorder could be helped. Blake most of all, for he saw a more confident, wonderfully radiant woman emerging as each day went by.

Yet it frightened him, too, he admitted as he came out of the ocean one afternoon and lay down on the towel he'd spread on the sand. He'd been exercising daily, trying to get back into shape, and getting a tan, anxious to be rid of the hospital pallor that lingered. Burned areas, he knew, didn't tan, and even the small scars on his back stood out starkly white on his darkening skin. Still, he thought he looked healthier than before.

Alone mornings, he'd gaze at his body in the mirror, trying to picture himself through Jenny's eyes. His left cheek was still reddened and blotchy, with one thick keloid scar crisscrossing the area. His left leg was more frail than his right, with several surgical scars, and his rebuilt kneecap was functional but unsightly in his own view. How was it that Jenny could care about the man he'd become? he asked himself continually.

Yet she seemed to do just that. She glowed with her newly discovered sensuality, kissing him frequently, touching him often, eager to make love with him regularly. As from the beginning, his imperfections seemed not to bother her. But they bothered the hell out of him.

Other thoughts bothered him also. Like reflections on the future. He couldn't spend the rest of his life lying on a Florida beach, resigned to a life of hiding from the world. But what did he want to do, if flying was no longer an option?

Blake sat up, staring out to sea. He wanted to teach. Even the little time he spent helping Jenny he enjoyed immensely. He didn't need two powerful legs to teach, nor an unscarred face. Maybe he'd look into the teaching requirements in Florida at the high school level. He certainly had no interest in returning to Michigan.

He liked Florida. Besides, it was where Jenny lived. Small towns were nice, comfortable, neighborly. But a question nagged at him. Would Jenny remain here once she could read well? She was bright and curious. Would she want to go on to college, to travel, to see something of the world? He certainly hadn't the right to ask her to stay if she wanted to go. No words of commitment had ever been spoken between them.

And that was the way he wanted it, Blake reminded himself.

Getting to his feet, Blake picked up his towel and started back to the cottage. The sun was high overhead. Jenny would be arriving soon. Depressed by his uneasy thoughts, he trudged home.

The phone was ringing. Hoping it wasn't Jenny canceling her trip over, Blake rushed to grab it.

"Hello, Blake," the voice said over the long-distance lines. "It's Frank Ambrose in San Antonio. I was about to hang up. How are you?"

Blake sat down, picturing the intense army surgeon from Brooks Medical Center who'd literally taken him from death's door to where he was now. He'd spent eighteen months doing everything Frank had asked of him. He had a strong feeling that Frank was calling now to ask him to do more. "I was out swimming. I'm coming along, Major. How are you?"

"Fine. How's the leg?"

"I broke my cane several weeks ago and never replaced it. The knee still gives me some trouble, but otherwise I'm all right."

"Your face must be healed also by now, especially if you're swimming in saltwater."

"Yeah. The ocean's great. You ought to come visit, take a vacation from all that blood and gore." It was an obvious attempt to distract the doctor from his condition, though Blake doubted it would work.

"I talked with Chet yesterday," Frank went on, ignoring the invitation. "He tells me you're ready for the last of the corrective surgery."

Blake felt his jaw tighten. "Physically maybe. Mentally I never want to see the inside of another hospital."

Frank's tone became a shade more reasonable. "I understand. It's the only way to correct that limp, Blake. And to minimize the pain in your knee."

"Yeah, well, I'll think about it."

"Wouldn't want to see you limp down the aisle."

That brought him up short. "What are you talking about?"

"Chet tells me you've met a woman there, someone you care about."

From the ashtray Blake picked up a silver ball and gripped it hard in his fist. "Chet's seeing things that aren't there. No one's walking down any aisles around here."

There was a short pause before Frank spoke again. "When they first brought you in here, almost two years ago now, you were burned and torn up pretty badly. Yet you were one hell of a fighter, never giving up. What happened, Blake?"

Blake sighed heavily. "Life happened, Frank. And life isn't always pretty."

"No, it's not. And I'm not going to give you a lot of crap about more surgery not being tough or painful. But, as a pilot, you were taught to evaluate each situation and make a decision based on your knowledge and experience. A man has to do that in life, too, Blake. Question is, can you?"

Blake slumped back in the chair. "I don't know."

"You know, all right, Blake. You know you need to get on with your life, to let us fix your leg and free you of constant pain, to get the plastic surgery done on your face so you won't feel the need to hide. I agreed that you should go to Apaloosa so you could rest and recover, not to bury yourself."

"Apaloosa's good enough for Chet."

"It's good enough for you, too, if you make a conscious choice to live there after you're whole and well. But not as a place to escape. Doesn't that woman you care about deserve to have you at your best?"

He felt the anger rise now, hot and heavy. "Let's leave her out of this, okay?"

"That's right, Blake. Get mad—at me, at Chet, at all of us. Then get over here and let me fix you up once and for all."

But would it be once and for all, or would there then be another, and still another, minor thing to clear up? He'd always had trouble winning discussions with Frank Ambrose. Still, he had a right to make his own decision on this one. "Is that an order, Major?"

"We don't usually order men into surgery. Hell, I can't even pull rank on you anymore."

"As I said, I'll give it some thought."

"You do that."

"Thanks for calling." Blake hung up the phone and felt like throwing it against the wall.

Hearing a car turn into his drive, he looked out the window. Moira was dropping Jenny off. Hurriedly he made his way to the shower. He needed a little time before facing her. She seemed to have far less trouble reading his moods than she had reading the pages of a book.

And he didn't need someone else on his back, too.

* * *

Elated, Jenny laughed out loud and closed the book. "The whole thing, Blake. I read the whole thing. I realize it's only fourth-grade level, but can you imagine?"

"Quite a lot of progress in three weeks, I'd say." He slipped his arm around her slender shoulders and drew her closer to him on the couch. "Pleased with yourself, are you?"

"Roberta's just great. She teaches by phonetics first, then we moved to the regular books. And she's *so* patient. I'm a long way from graduation, but I'm pleased with the results so far. And I have you to thank for making me do it."

He kissed the tip of her nose. "You're welcome."

"And I might even qualify for a GED diploma. There's an equivalency test that's given, and if you pass it, they give you your high school diploma. Roberta thinks that by winter, for sure, I'll be ready to take it."

His fingers got lost in her hair as he angled her more comfortably into his side. "You're no longer afraid of being tested?"

Jenny thought that over. "I'm not comfortable with the thought, but Roberta says she'll drill me ahead of time and won't let me take it until she's certain I'm prepared. She's a wonderful teacher." She raised her eyes to his. "I'll bet you're a wonderful teacher, as well."

"I've been thinking of looking into the teaching requirements here. Do you like living in Apaloosa?"

"I can scarcely remember living in Fort Lauderdale. I was pretty young and mostly so unhappy there that I think I've blocked it all out."

"Are you going to tell your father that you can read?"

"Maybe after I pass a few tests and am more sure of myself."

"It would shock the hell out of Jocelyn, wouldn't it?"

"I guess there's a part of me that would love to rub it in to her that I'm not retarded, that I can read and write as well as she. Not very nice of me, eh?"

"No, but very understandable. I don't think I could resist telling her."

Jenny shrugged. "Then again, what's to be gained? I still don't want anything to do with her."

"How about him?"

"My feelings about him are all tangled. I feel I should love him because he's my father. Yet he wasted no time in accepting Jocelyn's assessment of me. I've often wondered if he'd have had me put in an institution if Aunt Moira hadn't come up with an alternative."

He cupped her chin and raised her face to his. "No use dwelling on that. You'll never know."

She nodded. "You're right. Why did you ask if I like it here? Are you thinking of returning to Michigan?"

"I've already decided I don't want to return there. But I thought that you might not want to remain here. You might want to move after you go through this intensified education program."

Jenny frowned thoughtfully. "I don't think learning to read will change me, Blake. Except perhaps to make me happy about not feeling dumb."

He ran his hands along her arms. "Knowledge always changes people, Jenny."

"Not inside. Not what they are as a person."

"All right, then, tell me. What is it you think you might want to do once you have more options and opportunities to explore? Surely over the past few weeks you've thought about it."

"A little." Suddenly evasive, she dropped her gaze and concentrated on fiddling with the third button on his shirt.

Again he touched her face, so she had no choice but to look at him. "Tell me."

"I don't know exactly."

He'd started this, and now he would finish. Though he dreaded to hear her answers, he had to know. "What about going on to college? What about a career? Back when you accepted being unable to read, what was it you'd yearned to do that you felt you'd never be able to?"

She swallowed. "Blake, I'm finding this very hard to talk about."

Why? he wondered. Then the answer came. She was too kind to want to hurt him by saying she had her eye on a target he couldn't follow her to. She would have her restrictions removed, and he'd still have his. He should feel relief that she wanted no pledges or promises from him. Instead, he felt the sharp stab of disappointment. Blake eased back from her. "I understand."

Jenny studied his bent head. No, he didn't understand, not a word of what she was trying to say. She would have to spell it out, difficult as it would be. "From my earliest memory, what I wanted was someone to love, someone who would love me just as much." She watched him raise his head to look at her. "I didn't think anyone would or could love someone who was unteachable, but the dream wouldn't die. Then I met you." She touched his face, his dear face. "You ask what I want. My dream hasn't changed. It's just finally focused on a person. I want you."

He had trouble grasping, believing. "But what about the other things I mentioned—a career, college, travel?"

She placed a finger on his lips. "Shh. Those things would be nice perhaps. But in my heart all I want is to be with you." She faltered then, needing to ease his mind. "I know that what I want may not be what you want. And that's all right. There are no strings attached to this. I would never press you. But since you asked . . ."

Blake could stand it no longer. His arms pulled her closer, his mouth closed over hers. He hadn't dared admit his need for Jenny even to himself, yet she'd said the words he'd been longing to hear. His lips moved over hers, their breaths mingling, their hearts beating in unison. Never had he known such compelling need.

Breaking from her, he fought for control. "If it wasn't such a teenage thing to do, I'd shove that table aside and fall to the floor with you right here."

She smiled. "I think I missed out on a lot in my teens. No time like the present to remedy that." With her foot she pushed the coffee table out of the way, took his hand and rose with him. Feeling uncharacteristically driven, Jenny yanked open his shirt and ran her hands over his chest, then pressed her mouth to his throat. "I want you, Blake, only you." Hands encircling his neck, she pulled his mouth down to hers.

Her assault on his body left him breathless. She was all flash and fire, her busy hands stripping his clothes from him while her mouth never left his. He found her movements gloriously exciting as she rid herself of her own clothing while still keeping their lips joined. Then she was coaxing him to the carpet.

She was everything he'd dreamed of, her hands and mouth and tongue racing over every inch of him, an erotic journey that had him all but helpless. When her fingers closed over him, he heard his own groan of pleasure and then her delighted chuckle.

But it was time to take over, Blake decided, and rolled her onto her back, following her down. He would make this night memorable for both of them, for she'd given him more than he'd ever thought to have. He'd taken her innocence one night, but in many ways she'd given his back to him. She'd made him believe again that anything was possible.

He forgot all his reservations about the future, forgot that pain kept him from so many physical things he wanted to do. All of that slid into the background as he came flesh to flesh with Jenny, mouth to mouth with Jenny, heart to heart with Jenny. He felt her hands clutch his back, holding on, staking a claim. Her scent as always captivated him, drawing him in, making his head swim. Her taste was on his tongue as, fast and furious, he skimmed down her restless body.

Jenny heard an owl call to a mate through the open window as she arched to give Blake better access to all her secret places. She felt defenseless, yet not vulnerable. She felt needs throbbing inside that only he could assuage. She felt desire career through her system, and she heard herself whisper his name.

Suddenly she sensed his urgency and matched his demand. Tonight there would be no slow journey to fulfillment. Tonight she would throw caution to the four winds, for she needed him to know how her love knew no bounds. Tonight she would take a chance and love him as she'd longed to do. Swiftly and surely, she took him inside her.

Now his arms were around her and they were flying together, racing over new territory. Stunned at her abandon, Blake took control and ripped away hers. Patience had fled and passion had begun.

"Open your eyes," he ordered in a ragged breath. "I want to see your eyes."

Jenny did and found his penetrating gaze locked with hers. Moving with him, climbing with him, her eyes dark with desire, she held on. He lowered then to take her mouth, swallowing her swift cry of release as she whirled out of control. Drenched and damp, she wound her arms tightly around him and let the madness take her.

Aeons later, when he could move again, Blake lifted his head and touched her face. "This is all I want, too. Just you and I together and to hell with the rest of the world." Contentedly he buried his face in her throat.

As her heartbeat slowed, Jenny frowned. Something wasn't quite right. Blake was still hiding; only now he was hiding with her.

Chapter Ten

Blake sat back in the uncomfortable folding chair and waited. Off to one side of the driver's license testing room, Jenny was hunched over, reading the questions on the form. Her face was a study in concentration. She just had to pass this test, he thought as he glanced out the window.

He'd helped her study the preparation booklet until they both had memorized nearly the whole thing. He'd also taken her out driving daily for the past two weeks. She was ready, he was certain. Still, he worried.

It wouldn't be such a setback for the average person to miss a few questions and have to come back and retake the test another time. But for Jenny, Blake knew it would be a real blow to her self-confidence, and he'd hate to see that happen.

On the other hand, if she didn't get her license today, she wouldn't give up, he knew. She was determined to make up for the lost years. He saw a strength in her that he'd only glimpsed before as she studied her lessons with Roberta Ames, preparing for the upcoming GED test. She never complained, never let her work slide, either, keeping up his house as well as continuing to help out Dr. Swain. She had an amazing energy that Blake envied.

Actually, his own energy seemed in greater supply of late. Perhaps it was the exercises he performed religiously in and out of the water. He'd forced himself to go shopping and purchase weights, gradually increasing his workouts, strengthening his body. His appetite had increased and he'd filled out almost to his weight before the crash. Perhaps his feeling of fitness had something to do with Jenny's loving attention, as well, he admitted.

Though he'd asked, she hadn't moved in with him. She'd said it would shock their small-town neighbors and disappoint Aunt Moira, and she was probably right. But living apart from him didn't prevent her from returning to his bed regularly and often. She was wonderfully responsive and cleverly inventive for someone who hadn't been kissed for her first twenty-five years. It gave Blake enormous pleasure to be the first man to lead her down the sensual road of discovery.

Stretching out his long legs, he decided he was the happiest he'd been in years. Not just since the crash, but even before it. He'd also been doing some thinking about the future. After Jenny convinced him that she was content to be with him wherever he wanted to be, he'd thought that leaving Apaloosa just now might be a mistake. He'd grown fond of the small-town life and had considered making it home.

He'd written to the local school board, inquiring about teaching positions. By fall he would likely be strong enough for the long, grueling day of a teacher. With his permanent disability income and family money he had invested, he really didn't need to work, but he wanted to feel useful again.

Last week, while Jenny had been with Roberta, he'd gone for a drive, looking at beach property. He'd found a lot for sale that would be perfect to build a house on. A special home where the two of them could close off the rest of the world. If Jenny wanted to work at something that made her happy, that would be up to her. If she chose to stay home, that would be fine, too. He'd be pleased if she were.

Life, perhaps, held some meaning after all, Blake thought as he turned back to check on Jenny.

On the way home from the testing center that evening Blake unexpectedly pulled up near the awning-covered entrance of McGuire's, a popular seafood restaurant in nearby Hollywood.

"What a nice surprise," Jenny exclaimed, equally as pleased with her ability to read the sign as she was to be going out to dinner.

"I thought we'd celebrate your passing the test."

Since he was in an expansive mood, Jenny decided to take a risk. "Blake, would you take the bandage off your cheek, please?"

He hesitated, annoyed because she knew how he felt about having people see his uncovered face. Yet she asked so little of him. Silently he reached up and removed the bandage. Her thankful smile as they walked in warmed him.

It was early and the dining room wasn't terribly crowded. Blake tried to minimize his limp as a waiter sporting a bushy mustache led them to a table by a bank of windows that looked out on the sea. He lit twin candles, then left them while Jenny pored over the menu.

Candlelight flickered in her hair, shadowing her face. She was so lovely, so happy, Blake thought. He had noticed a man at the door and one at a nearby table look her over appreciatively as they'd walked in. Then both had glanced at him, surprise registering in their eyes. Beauty and the beast, they'd probably said to themselves.

With his hand curled around his left cheek, he looked out the window. The lowering sun shimmered on the water's surface. Tourists walked along a small overpass bridge in the distance. A woman's low laugh came from somewhere behind him and a piano tinkled in the background. A perfect evening, a perfect setting.

Then why did he feel like running?

Coming here was a mistake, Blake decided as he picked up the menu and hid behind its generous width. He hadn't been in a public restaurant in over two years. He felt awkward, conspicuous, uneasy.

Jenny looked around, pleased to be eating out. "Are you sure I'm dressed all right for this place?" she asked, glancing down at her yellow cotton dress.

"You look wonderful," he told her honestly.

She smiled then and turned to study the menu. "How does crab-stuffed sole sound?" Jenny asked.

When he didn't answer or lower his menu, she reached to touch his hand. "Blake?"

"Yeah, sounds good."

The waiter reappeared. "Would you care to see a wine list, sir?"

"Thanks." Blake took the leather folder and glanced inside. "Something white and tart..." He looked up in time to catch the sympathy in the man's eyes as the waiter stared at his face.

Recovering, the waiter coughed into his fist. "May I suggest number 26, sir. Very nice."

"Fine." Blake handed him the list and turned back to the window as the waiter went for the wine.

Jenny leaned forward. "Is something wrong?"

Why had he been stupid enough to think everything was fine simply because he was out with a beautiful woman who seemed to care for him? Briefly he closed his eyes on the thought. "Yeah, I'm wrong. All wrong."

She reached for his hand again, found it closed in a tense fist. He was feeling self-conscious, she knew, and wished she could ease his discomfort. "You're not wrong and no one's looking at us."

He gave a short laugh. "No, they're trying very hard to *not* look at us once they've had a glimpse of me."

"That's ridiculous. You know, most people are interested in their own lives, not in the lives of others."

"Most people are curious as hell about people who are different."

"Do you want to leave?"

At that moment the waiter returned and poured wine into Blake's glass. Blake tasted it and nodded his approval. "Let's order," he said to Jenny while the waiter finished pouring. Damn, he hadn't meant to spoil her day.

After they gave their order, he raised his glass. "I'm sorry, Jenny. Here's to another victory, your driver's license."

She picked up her glass, clinked it to his and took a sip. But her heart wasn't in it. Was this how he'd be every time they left the cottage? She ached for him, but there was so little she could do or say to ease his misery.

"I found something last week I want to show you later. Surprise number two." Maybe he could salvage the evening by telling her about the lot.

She gave him a hopeful smile. "What is it?"

"A piece of property on the southeastern tip of Apaloosa. About ten acres of citrus trees plus this section on a hill that faces the sea. It's quiet and beautiful and private."

Her eyes were steady on his. "What about it?"

"It'd be a great place to build a house. Nearest neighbor about five miles away. You could swim in the ocean in the raw."

Jenny found herself smiling through a blush. "I could, eh? And what would you be doing while I was swimming?"

Blake smiled back. "Watching you."

"Why, Major, you're a dirty old man. So, then, you've decided to stay in Apaloosa?"

"A while back, you said all you wanted was to be with me. If you like that piece of land and I buy it and we design a house together to build on it, would you stay with me?"

Jenny's eyes widened. "My, you certainly know how to knock a woman off guard, now don't you?"

Blake ran a finger around the rim of his wineglass, wondering if he shouldn't have waited to bring up this conversation. Or perhaps not have had it at all. "You did say something about wanting to be with me. Or have you changed your mind?"

She shook her head, giving him a tolerant smile. "You can be such a pouty little boy sometimes. No, I haven't changed my mind, nor will I."

The waiter cleared his throat, drawing their attention to his renewed presence. As they both sat back, he served their dinners. "Will there be anything else just now?"

"Thank you, no." Blake took a forkful and found the sole delicious. "As I was saying, it's been my understanding that people who care about each other often want to live together."

Jenny sampled the fish and tasted disappointment. "Live together," she repeated.

"Isn't that what you want?" Blake swallowed more wine. This wasn't turning out to be nearly as simple as he'd thought.

Toying with her food, Jenny searched for the right words. "I told you that as long as I can remember, I wanted someone of my own to love. But I don't ever recall wishing that my Prince Charming would simply ask me to live with him."

He should have guessed. The very word *love* scared him to death. Yet he did care for her, deeply. And now she wanted even more. "You want the paperwork. You want marriage."

"Only because of the children."

Blake's head shot up. "Children?"

Jenny set down her fork. "You don't like children?"

"I haven't been around them much, but I suppose I do." He was thoughtful for a moment, picturing a little girl with Jenny's blue eyes and her laugh. "Okay, children." He drained his glass. "I suppose then we could get married."

Jenny sighed. "And I suppose that there have been more romantic proposals in the history of recorded time."

He had the decency to look chagrined. Reaching out, he took her hand. "I'm not good at this."

"You'll get no argument from me on that."

"I wanted to tell you about the lot and the house and then things snowballed. I didn't know we'd get to this part tonight, or I...I would have gone about it differently." Her dark blue eyes just stared into his, and he saw she wasn't going to help him this time. Blake cleared his throat. "Jenny Starbuck, I love you. Will you marry me?"

She smiled then, radiantly, and gripped his fingers. "Will you tell me why we're here in the midst of strangers having the most important discussion of our lives? I don't want to eat. I want to go somewhere private and hold you, kiss you."

Things were moving a little fast for him, but he *had* started this subject. Blake signaled the waiter for their check.

It took far too long to convince the man that they really weren't hungry. Jenny skipped outside, too excited to wait as Blake paid the bill. It was twilight and the front parking lot was filled with cars, but few people were outside. Restless with anticipation, Jenny moved alongside the Mustang.

Two young collegiate-looking men pulled up several car lengths away and got out. The driver, tall and blond, eyed Jenny as he approached.

"All alone, little lady?" he asked. "How about joining us?"

Jenny shook her head. "No, thanks."

The blonde's curly-haired companion ambled closer, his dark eyes appreciative as they looked her over. "Come on, honey. A little dinner, then we go on to Pogo Pete's and dance a little. We're renting a condo on the beach and we're harmless."

The blond man laughed.

"I'm with someone," Jenny said more firmly. "Thanks, anyway." She looked toward the walk and saw Blake coming toward them, pocketing his wallet.

Reaching her side, he withdrew his keys as he glanced at the men who were now studying him. Slowly they turned and started for the restaurant entrance.

"Look at old scarface, will you?" the blonde commented. "Must be filthy rich, or a babe like that wouldn't give him a second glance."

As the two men burst into laughter, Blake's face grew stormy and he clenched his hands into fists.

Jenny touched his arm. "Don't let them upset you. They're just kids."

Still seething, Blake unlocked the Mustang and got behind the wheel.

Feeling his pain, Jenny got in beside him. She looked over as he turned the key. "Blake?"

"I don't want to talk right now, okay?" Jerking into reverse, he backed up, then roared out of the parking lot.

Swallowing around a lump in her throat, Jenny stared down at her hands twisted together in her lap. How could they go from a happy celebration to an uncomfortable silence so quickly?

He took a shortcut back and arrived in Apaloosa in record time. Blake kept his foot steady on the gas, passing whenever he approached a car, scarcely noticing that Jenny's face seemed drained of color and that she clutched her hands together in a white-knuckled grip. He was too upset to care and too angry to talk. As he pulled into her drive, he hoped she would quietly leave and allow him to go home and get over his black mood in private.

The motor idling, he stared stone-faced out the front window, waiting for her to get out of the car.

What should she say? Jenny wondered. What *could* she say? She'd struggled to think of something, *anything,* yet nothing she thought of seemed right. Heart pounding in her throat, she turned toward him and went with her instincts. "Thank you for dinner. I'll see you tomorrow."

"No." Blake coughed into his fist. "I have something I need to do tomorrow. I'll . . . call you."

She wouldn't plead with him, even though the tears rushed to her eyes. He was proud and stubborn and used to going it alone. Jenny understood that. "Good night, then." Quickly she left him and went inside her silent, empty house.

Blake sat for a moment, staring up at a darkening sky and a full lover's moon. What a laugh! Disgusted with himself and the way he'd treated Jenny, he pulled out of the drive and headed for the haven of his cottage. At least alone there would be no prying eyes filled with sympathy, no shocked ladies averting their gaze from him, no young punks ridiculing.

In the kitchen he opened the cupboard and reached for the bottle of whiskey without turning on the light. He poured a hefty shot and tossed it back, grimacing as the liquor burned its way down his throat. He'd never been much of a drinker, his commitment to flying and keeping in shape always uppermost on his mind. Maybe it was time he gave it a try. He poured another splash into the glass.

Mr. No-nose came sauntering in and jumped up onto the counter, eyeing him warily. In the dim moonlight coming in the window, Blake examined the cat's battered face. He, too, was healed, as Blake was. And they both looked a pitiful sight.

Picking up his drink, Blake scooped the cat into his free arm. "Come on, you scruffy thing. Let's see if what they say about alcohol making the pain go away is true." Somewhat unsteadily, he walked over and slumped down onto the living room couch.

They lied. Blake opened his eyes to bright morning sunshine, rolled over and groaned. Not only did alcohol not take away pain, it increased it.

Stomach rolling, head pounding, he hobbled to the bathroom. Aspirin and two glasses of water helped a little. A long, hot shower made him feel almost human. Almost.

He put on the coffee and looked out the window, staring out to sea. Drinking, alone or otherwise, cured nothing, he decided. Obviously he had needed to prove that to himself last night. Or had he instead merely been feeling sorry for himself? Probably the latter, he thought with an impatient sigh.

A movement on the beach caught his eye. Someone out walking with a dog alongside. A woman in a dress blowing in the breeze. Jenny? Too far to make out who it was. No, not Jenny. She'd be at her studies with Roberta this morning. Her mind would probably be troubled though, remembering last night.

His thoughts were troubled also, Blake acknowledged as he poured himself a cup of coffee. He'd asked her to marry him, then lost his temper and treated her shabbily. She didn't deserve that. Hadn't he said all along that Jenny Starbuck deserved a better man than he?

Blake finished the coffee quickly despite the heat, needing the caffeine jolt. Pouring another, he decided he also needed to get out of the house. Maybe if he visited with men for a while, men like the man he'd once been, his perspective would return.

Lieutenant Tom Payne was at Homestead Air Force Base only an hour's drive south. Tom had invited him to visit anytime. Maybe there, back on familiar military territory, he could face his past, put to rest his impossible dreams and accept his fate. Crossing the room, Blake picked up the phone.

He'd never been to Homestead, yet he felt at home immediately. All military bases were pretty much alike, Blake thought as he stood at the edge of the field, narrowing his eyes against the glare of the sun. It felt odd to be back in his summer uniform, but he'd felt it appropriate. The guard at the gate had given him a snappy salute, checked his ID, then called Lieutenant Tom Payne, who'd met him moments later. Standing beside him now, Blake felt Tom wondering what had brought him here so unexpectedly.

If he knew, he might have told Tom.

"Travis is here, too," Tom said, obviously wanting to break into Blake's thoughtful silence. "Got transferred only last week. I could track him down, have him meet us for a cup of coffee. He'd be glad to see you."

Lieutenant Travis McGill, another one of the pilots he'd trained. A good man with a sharp mind destined to go places. Blake didn't want to see him. "Some other time," he said, looking over the airfield. From the far left came the roar of a jet as it took off, streaking into the sky. He inhaled the familiar odor of burnt kerosene heavy in the thick air.

"Bring back a few memories?" Tom asked carefully.

Blake stuck his hands into his pant pockets. "Yeah, a few." He began to walk out onto the tarmac into the area where several planes were parked.

Uneasily Tom fell into step alongside. "Heard that your buddy, Grady, was discharged last month. One of the airlines snapped him up. I forget which one."

"Grady always said he'd fly domestic as soon as he got out," Blake commented. "That what you plan to do?"

"Nah, I'm in for the long haul. Career man."

"Good for you." Blake stopped in front of a T-38 and looked up. At least *they* hadn't changed.

Tom looked at his former trainer with a puzzled frown. "Let me ask you, Blake. Why'd you come out here today? You don't want to see any of the guys. I don't even think you came to see me. What is it?"

"Damned if I know." Blake pulled down the stairs of the T-38. "You always have a clear-cut reason for everything you do?"

"Mostly."

"You're a lucky guy." On the bottom step Blake shoved open the canopy opening. "I know it's probably against regulations, but I want to go up inside, just for a few minutes. I won't do anything stupid, so you can relax."

Tom looked anything but relaxed. He glanced around as if searching for someone in authority who would take the decision out of his hands, but no one else was nearby. "I guess it'd be all right," he muttered reluctantly.

Blake swung up inside and stood with his hand on the back of the pilot's seat. Memories flooded his mind of the first time he'd ever entered a cockpit, and that fateful day when he was last inside a T-38. Carefully he sat down in the leather seat. His right hand automatically gripped the stick, his left moving to grasp the throttle. His feet found the rudder pedals without his conscious effort.

His eyes skimmed the airspeed indicator dial, the altimeter and the attitude indicator. The needles were at rest, the plane grounded, the message mocking him. He looked out the windshield, but it wasn't the scene before him that he saw. It was a clear blue sky stretching endlessly before him broken only by streaks of white jet trails. He heard the whine of the powerful engines and smelled the jet exhaust fumes, that special pungency that permeated a pilot's clothes and hair.

Blake's eyes clouded as he let himself recall that last afternoon, the helplessness he'd felt when he faced the inevitability of a crash. His arms tensed and sweat beaded on his forehead as he pictured the field coming closer, closer. Black smoke had swirled around him, and he'd tasted real fear for the first time in his life. With a shudder Blake closed his eyes.

So many hours he'd spent in one of these, so many memories. Had he come to say goodbye? Blake wondered. The past was just that, past. Gone, irretrievable, lost forever. Only fools lived in the past, clung to it, longed for those days to return. Blake had never considered himself a fool. Yet here he was.

Suddenly annoyed with himself, he rose and stepped out. He saw Tom's troubled frown as he shoved the stairs up, then wiped his damp hands on his pants. The kid was too young to comprehend Blake's needs and confusion, too healthy and inexperienced to relate. "Sorry if I worried you."

"You didn't," Tom lied as relief replaced anxiety.

"Do you ever have nightmares about the crash?"

Tom nodded. "Not so much anymore, but often at first."

Blake started walking back. Here was the one man who'd lived through the nightmare with him. Surely he'd understand. "I hate to admit it, but remembering how scared I was almost paralyzes me sometimes."

"It was bad, but there are worse fears a man can face than his own death."

Stopping, Blake stared into Tom's clear blue eyes. "Really? Like what?"

"You remember I told you I have a son? Tommy was three this May. Last summer he managed to shove open a patio door and fall into our backyard pool. By the time we found him, I thought sure he was gone. He was turning blue as I gave him CPR. Somehow the paramedics revived him, and he's fine now, like nothing happened. I never want to experience something like that again. The possibility of losing someone you love, that's real fear.'' Tom squinted up at Blake. ''You don't have children, so you probably don't know what I mean, at least not yet.''

He'd never lost anyone he'd loved. Or had he? The memory of Jenny's pale face last night came to him, and he shuddered.

No, he didn't have children. But he did love someone who wanted to have children with him. Just the possibility of losing Jenny had his palms dampening again. And he'd all but thrown her love back in her face last night.

Blake reached to shake the young pilot's hand. ''Thanks.''

Tom gripped Blake's hand with both of his. ''Blake, I wish there was something I could say or do to help you. I know it must be tough adjusting to...to everything.''

''You *have* helped.'' The smile he gave Tom was genuine. ''I've got to go.'' Suddenly he was a man in a hurry.

Walking as quickly as possible, he rushed to his car. And prayed he wasn't too late.

She was scrubbing her kitchen floor. Blake stood on Moira's back porch and watched Jenny through the screen door. Not just scrubbing, but wielding the brush like a weapon, shoving the soapy lather around as if she needed to remove several years' accumulation of dirt. Her long hair was caught at her nape with a gold clip, the length trailing down the back of the long blue shirt she wore. Barefoot, down on her knees, her shorts-clad bottom rotated appealingly as she attacked the floor.

An Italian opera blared forth from the stereo, which was why she hadn't heard his car or his steps on the porch. Rafferty fidgeted at his feet, but Blake ignored the dog, fascinated by the sight of Jenny so obviously working off a bout of anger.

Was she angry with him for last night? He wouldn't blame her if she were. Yet she'd left him so quietly, so calmly. He'd never seen her give into temper and decided that, steaming, he found her particularly exciting.

Blake stepped inside. When he moved closer and bent to touch her arm, she reared back with a shriek, nearly losing her balance. He saw the surprise in her eyes be replaced by a wariness as she struggled to her feet on the slippery floor.

"I'm sorry," he said simply. "I behaved badly."

Her blue eyes were huge as they searched his. Her hand still held the brush, and she clung to it as if for support.

A shiver of fear raced through him. What if she didn't forgive him? He ran a shaky hand through his hair and tried again. "I hurt you," he said, thinking the words inadequate.

"Yes," Jenny said softly.

"I didn't mean to." He hadn't had to apologize often in his lifetime and knew he wasn't good at it. This time he would beg, plead, anything. He had to have her back. "Please forgive me."

She saw the uncertainty, the worry he didn't bother to hide. With a muffled sob she dropped the brush and moved into his embrace.

Releasing a trembling breath, Blake's arms went around her, holding her tightly to him, his face in the silk of her hair.

She spoke against his chest. "You keep shutting me out. I don't know what to say or do, how to reach you."

"I know and I'm sorry." Emotions churned, clawed at him. Tom was right. The fear of losing Jenny was greater than the fear he'd felt as his plane had hurtled toward the earth. "I love you."

At last the words she'd been longing to hear. Jenny kissed him, letting him feel all the love she had stored up for him.

She was a mixture of strength and vulnerability, and he needed to remember that second part. Needed to try harder not to hurt her again. Pulling back, Blake touched her face. "I can't promise it won't ever happen again. I can promise you I'll try."

"Why won't you believe that you're as good as anyone, better than most, and nearly everyone thinks so? Let those who don't be damned. I had to learn that a long time ago. The most perfect of people are criticized sometimes. You make things so difficult for yourself, Blake." She shifted to place a soft kiss in the palm of his hand.

The gesture moved him and so did her words. "And difficult for you, too, I know. I'll be better, Jenny." He swallowed hard, needing to say more, wishing he didn't. "Just don't walk away from me, please."

She blinked the tears back. "As if I could." On a soft moan she rose on tiptoe and pressed her mouth to his. Opening to him, she sent her tongue to join his, her hands gliding up to tangle in his hair.

The kiss went on and on as Blake poured his love into his touch. His hands slid over her sweet curves, molding her to him. He heard her breath catch in her throat as he cradled her to him intimately. He wanted her to be as weak as she made him. "I want to feel you against me, all of you," he murmured hoarsely as his lips moved down the satin column of her throat.

Linking her hands behind his neck, she smiled lazily. "In the middle of the day while the sun is shining?"

"Yes, right now, right here. I want to make love with you. I can't seem to stop wanting that."

Her eyes on his kindled, then flamed. Taking his hand, she led him down the hallway and into her bedroom. There, she rested her head a moment on his shoulder and closed her eyes.

He held her and briefly glanced around the room. It had none of the subtle elegance of his mother's room, nor the frilly disorder of Eleanor's. Like Jenny, it was honest, feminine and charming.

She had flowers in a pale blue vase, the same wildflowers she'd brought into his home. She had easy colors, broken only by a vivid painting on one wall showing a dark-haired child smelling flowers amid a riot of yellow buttercups. Her scent lingered on the white crocheted bedspread he laid her on.

Blake leaned down and kissed her with such gentleness that Jenny felt the room tilt. She sensed something new, something different in him, but she was too caught up to put a name to it. In moments the mists closed in and she began to drift.

His fingers were slow and a little clumsy as he unbuttoned her blouse and tugged off her shorts. The wooden blinds were slanted, the room in shadows as he slipped out of his clothes unhurriedly. Passion rising, she waited, anticipation racing through her. It never failed to amaze her how he could make her heart pound, her blood heat, her restless body crave more and still more.

Rejoining her, Blake heard the sounds of pleasure low in her throat as his mouth journeyed over her. At his leisure he explored every sensitive spot, each hollow and curve. His hands stroked, his mouth tasted, as she arched against his clever fingers. Taking her to the edge, he withdrew and directed his attention to the pulse that pounded in her throat.

He aroused and teased, making her climb higher and higher, then let her go limp only to return and arouse again. His hands never still, he wandered over her, no area common enough to escape his attention. In a frenzy, in a fever, she shifted restlessly under the assault of his greedy mouth.

Mellow loving rose to sharp urgency as their demands grew. Blake raised himself over her, wanting to watch her face as he made her his.

In the shadowy light her eyes came open, dark with need. This was the way he wanted it, the two of them alone, locked away from an unfriendly world. And Jenny thinking of no one but him; Jenny wanting no one but him; Jenny loving no one but him. "I love you," he whispered as he slipped into her and saw her eyes soften with the words she needed to hear.

Her hands tightened on his back as he moved slowly, then picked up the pace. He had her trembling as she climbed, weakening as she gazed up at him, gasping as he took her to the edge. Aching to end it, yet wanting the sensations to go on and on, Jenny clung to him.

Blake saw her face go dusky with passion as the pressure inside him built. Clinging to a tenuous control, he heard her whisper his name, then close her eyes as she jolted in his arms. He could have wept with the beauty of it.

At last he let himself join her, soaring with her to a place that only two lovers perfectly attuned could reach.

Feeling wonderfully sated, Blake leaned on his elbows and looked at Jenny. Her breathing had quieted and she lay still beneath him, but he knew she was awake. For the first time he noticed shadows in the fair skin under her eyes. Gently he brushed a finger along one cheek, then the other and saw her eyes open. "You haven't been sleeping well."

She did when she slept with him, which wasn't often enough. Jenny didn't think this was the right moment to tell him that. "I'm fine," she said, her hand caressing his back. She wiggled her hips suggestively. "More than fine."

He smiled, but the concern didn't leave his eyes. "I put those dark circles there. I'll make it up to you, Jenny."

"There's no need. I—"

The jolting ring of the bedside phone made her jump. So few people called, especially in the middle of the day. As Blake shifted his weight from her, she picked it up on the second ring.

"Jenny, it's Aunt Moira. I'm glad I found you. I'm at the library and I'll be heading home shortly."

There was an odd tone to her aunt's voice. Alarm skittered up Jenny's spine. "Is anything wrong?"

Moira Ryan sighed, as if she wished she could postpone the news. "It's Lucius. Jocelyn just phoned me. He's had a massive coronary."

"Oh, no." Her hand flew to her throat as she sat up. "How is he?"

"He's gone, lass."

Chapter Eleven

By the time Moira's car turned into her drive, Jenny and Blake had dressed and the kitchen floor had been haphazardly mopped. Jenny sat on the living room couch, wishing she could cry.

"Something's wrong with me that I can't weep for him." She spoke softly, as if to herself.

Blake took her hand. "He hurt you badly years ago and never bothered to heal the rift. It's understandable."

"Is it? I wonder." Jenny laced her fingers with his. "I should feel *something*. The only emotion I'm aware of is a heavy sadness that we couldn't have been closer, that I couldn't have been a daughter he could be proud of."

"You're far more generous than I'd be in the same situation," Blake countered. "The sad thing is that your father died without realizing how special you are."

Jenny smiled at him then. "I'd planned to let him know about my dyslexia. I'd fantasized about driving up to his home and showing off my new reading and writing skills." She swallowed past a lump in her throat. "I waited too long."

"Don't blame yourself." Blake heard the back screen door slam shut and Moira Ryan enter. "I should go. You two have things to discuss."

She gripped his hand harder. "No, stay, please."

Moira Ryan paused in the archway, a weary slump to her shoulders. "Good afternoon, Major."

Blake wasn't sure why Moira insisted on the formality. "Hello, Miss Ryan," he said, answering in kind. He watched her assess the scene. Her wise blue eyes seemed to notice more than many might have.

Moira stepped closer to Jenny. "Are you all right, lass?"

"Yes, but I can't seem to truly mourn him, Aunt Moira." She still held Blake's hand as if clinging to a lifeline.

With a sigh Moira eased into her bentwood rocker and patted the coiled braids at the back of her head. "Now don't you be blaming yourself that you can't cry for the man, Jenny. You and I both did our grieving years ago when we left Lucius Starbuck's home."

"I suppose. How's Jocelyn holding up?"

Moira gave a disgusted snort. "She's likely out shopping for a new black dress," she said, then glanced heavenward as if asking forgiveness for such an uncharitable remark. "We'll not waste our time worrying about that one."

"At least it was over quickly and he didn't suffer long, right?" She hadn't loved the man, but she hadn't wanted him to be hurting, either.

"So I was told. The services are to be day after tomorrow. It appears that Jocelyn's anxious to be rid of him." Moira's eyes wandered to Blake, as if belatedly remembering there was a stranger in their midst. "I'm sorry to be airing our dirty laundry in front of you, Major. But, then, I believe you have more than a passing interest in our family."

She was from Ireland, old-fashioned and traditional, he supposed. Was she waiting for him to ask her for her niece's hand now that her father was no longer alive? The thought amused Blake, yet made him a shade nervous, as well. Suppose Moira had wanted better for Jenny than a man of his limitations?

But Jenny wanted him, Blake reminded himself. He'd have to hold on to that thought. Still, this was neither the time nor the place to discuss his interest in Jenny. Yet Moira seemed to be waiting for his reply. "You could say that, yes."

Moira nodded as if she'd known what his answer would be. "I much prefer weddings over funerals, but we'll need to go pay our respects to your father, Jenny. For now I think I'll take a short rest." She stood, rubbing her back as if it ached. "I don't suppose the two of you will mind if I leave you alone."

Jenny watched her aunt walk down the hall. At her niece's door Moira paused to glance in and undoubtedly noticed the rumpled bedding Jenny hadn't had time to fix. Neatness was a habit deeply ingrained in Jenny, so Moira must have guessed why her bed was unmade in the middle of the day. Jenny raised her chin a fraction, waiting. She wouldn't apologize for loving Blake if her aunt chose to censure her. The house was hers as well as Moira's. But Moira passed on by and went into her own room, closing the door.

Jenny let out a relieved breath and moved into Blake's arms.

He nuzzled her cheek. "Did you think she needed proof?" He gazed at her mouth still swollen from his kisses, her face with that well-loved glow despite the shock she'd received. "She knew the moment she walked in. Does that bother you?"

"I've always been a private person. She never comes home at midday so I thought . . . well, it doesn't matter." She smiled and ran a finger along the fullness of his lower lip. "I think she might have been thinking that I was going through my first real crush—until today."

He nibbled at the corner of her mouth. "Are you?"

"I've had a few crushes, usually unattainable men I've admired from a distance." Her eyes grew serious. "But I've known only one love."

Blake kissed her, gently at first, then more heatedly. But he was uncomfortably aware that they weren't really alone, so he drew back and touched Jenny's cheek. "I'm going to go and let you two make your plans. Will you be leaving tomorrow?"

She went very still. "Aren't you coming with me?"

Blake frowned. "Why would I? I didn't know your father, and I don't know Jocelyn."

"I just thought you'd go. I'd feel better."

Sighing, he took her hands in his. "Jenny, I'm not good with strangers. You know that."

"Yes, I do know that. I also know you have to get over your reluctance to be with people. You told me you were going to try."

"I *am* trying. You have to give me time." Annoyed, he stood. "It's not as if you need me on this trip. I see no point in going." He moved toward the door, suddenly anxious to be gone.

"All right." Jenny followed him into the kitchen.

Feeling guilty, Blake swung back to her and saw the disappointment on her face. Damn, but he didn't need this. "Call me when you get back," he said curtly. She didn't answer. Fighting a rising anger, he left with a bang of the screen door.

Jenny stood there for several minutes, her forehead resting on the doorframe, listening to his car pull away. He'd come looking for her to apologize and she'd melted in his arms. Now they were back to square one, on opposite sides of the same old issue.

Would it always be like this between them? she wondered.

Jenny sat in the front row of the old church, her eyes dry and her heart heavy. The priest said mass, offering comfort along with the ancient ceremony. She wondered if the man in the flag-draped coffin was at peace finally. Lucius Starbuck had always seemed a restless, driven man to her.

Across the aisle his widow, shrouded in expensive black silk, sat surrounded by a bevy of her Fort Lauderdale friends. At regular intervals she dabbed daintily at her eyes and accepted a pat on the hand from a white-haired man seated on her right. Since a somewhat frosty greeting at the door, Jocelyn hadn't said a word to either Jenny or Moira.

The church was nearly full, Jenny noted with surprise. A testimony perhaps to Lucius's business activities and his wife's social involvements more than to the fact that her father had been greatly loved. Over the years she'd become aware that her father had inspired respect more often than love.

At the tinkle of bells the mourners shifted to kneel. As Jenny moved forward, she saw that next to her, her aunt's eyes were wet with tears. Leaning closer, she put her arm around Moira's thin shoulders.

"I keep wondering," Moira said very quietly, "what he'd have been like had your mother lived."

"Very different, I'm sure," Jenny answered. At least she liked to think so. Bowing her head, she offered prayers for both her parents.

She'd heard the story often of how deeply in love Annie Ryan and Lucius Starbuck had been. Yet the course of that love hadn't run smoothly, with his business travels separating them frequently, then having to cope with Annie's illness and a difficult child. Were such problems the norm for every couple? Jenny wondered. She hadn't witnessed many marriages firsthand. And here she was contemplating her own.

She wished Blake had come with her. She could use his strength, his quiet support. Recently she'd fantasized about taking Blake to meet her father, perhaps asking him to wear the uniform she'd seen in his closet. Lucius had been in the military, too. She had hoped it would have provided them a common ground. But it wasn't to be. Jenny closed her eyes briefly on the thought.

She would be proud to have him beside her right now, just as he was. But she knew he didn't believe that. Would he ever? Could love stay alive if kept hidden away in the shadows—two people never walking together in the sunshine, never holding their heads high? She hadn't enough experience to even guess.

Finally the mass ended and Jocelyn left her pew to pause at the casket briefly. With a muffled sob she turned and quickly left. Jenny stood silently watching Lucius Starbuck's neighbors, friends and business associates file past and say their farewells. She stepped back then and let Aunt Moira pay her respects.

Alone at last, she walked slowly forward and placed her hand on the polished brass handle of her father's final resting place. For a moment she let herself remember the deep timbre of his voice, the richness of his laugh when she watched him as a child with her mother, the security and love she'd felt all too briefly in her early years. There had to have been some good times. She wished there had been more.

"I'm sorry, Father," Jenny whispered. "So very sorry." Curling her hand into a fist, she felt the tears come.

"Thank you, Jocelyn," Moira said as she stood at the foot of the church steps, "but Jenny and I need to be getting back."

"If you prefer," Jocelyn said, adjusting the veil of her smart black hat. "I've invited our closest friends back to the house for a bite to eat. If you can't make it, I understand."

Composed again, Jenny stepped down to where the two women stood, sensing her stepmother's relief that they wouldn't be joining the others. She touched Moira's arm. "We should go."

Jocelyn turned to look more carefully at her husband's only child. "You look different somehow, Jenny. Are you still having your...seizures?"

Jenny struggled to keep her face expressionless. "I never had seizures, Jocelyn. They were temper tantrums."

"Mmm. What do you do with yourself all day, locked up in that house while Moira's at work?"

"Oh, I have my coloring books and crayons, my building blocks." She felt a jolt of satisfaction as Jocelyn's brown eyes filled with suspicion. Raising her chin, Jenny tugged at Moira's arm. "The car's this way." Without another word she hustled her aunt away.

By the time they reached the car, Moira was nearly sputtering. "That wasn't very nice, Jenny. Not at all the way I brought you up."

"You're right." She opened the car door and smiled. "But it felt awfully good." She was about to get in when she heard someone call her name.

"Wait, Jenny, please." The white-haired man who'd been sitting with Jocelyn hurried over. Stopping in front of Jenny, he smiled pleasantly. "You don't remember me, do you?"

He looked vaguely familiar, but she couldn't put a name to him. "No, I'm sorry, I don't."

"I'm Henry Blanchard, your father's attorney." He glanced back toward the church. "Lucius and I have been friends for thirty years. I shall miss him." Clearing his throat, Henry turned back and handed a card to Jenny. "Here's my office address. I'll need you to be there at noon next Monday."

Jenny stared at the card, puzzled. "What for?"

"For the reading of your father's will." He included Moira in his invitation. "You'll want to be there, too, Miss Ryan."

"Of course. We will be, thank you." Moira got behind the wheel.

"Good, good." With a nod Henry turned and walked back to join Jocelyn, still standing by the church steps.

Across the narrow parking lot Jenny's eyes locked with her stepmother's cold gaze. She felt a shiver take her, then climbed in beside Moira. "I don't like that woman," she said, fastening her seat belt.

Moira started the car. "Really? You hide the fact so well."

Noticing her aunt's mouth twitch, Jenny smiled, then sobered quickly. Her father's will. That was one she hadn't thought of. "If my dear stepmother had anything to say about the will, I'll inherit some swampland in the Everglades and she'll get the rest."

Moira smiled. "Aye, and don't you be expecting more than that."

Always one to cushion the fall, Jenny thought as she rubbed her forehead. She so seldom had headaches, but then the past few days had been filled with stress. She'd had to deal with her father's death, Jocelyn's animosity and Blake's stubbornness.

"You didn't go to the major's cottage yesterday," Moira commented as she swung onto the highway. "Is there anything wrong between you?"

It wasn't in Jenny's nature to lie. "You could say that."

"I wouldn't have thought so by the look of the two of you when I came home that afternoon, nor by the state of your bedroom."

Jenny felt the heat rise. She was unused to confiding in her aunt about a man and didn't quite know how to go about it. "I've discovered that two people can be compatible in the bedroom and not see eye to eye on other things."

"Aye, and that's the truth of it. Your mother used to tell me the same thing."

The strange reference to her mother sparked Jenny's curiosity. "Was that so?"

"Yes, you know, your mother loved Lucius dearly, but he didn't always do right by her. Now there weren't any other women, mind you. It was more that to a man like Lucius, his work came first. A woman, *any* woman, had to settle for second place in his priorities. That hurt Annie, as it would most of us."

Jenny had to agree with that. "How did she handle my father when he took a stubborn stand on something and refused to see another way?"

"Ah, that woman. She just kept on loving him and letting him know she did. Any man worth loving, Annie used to say, has a great deal of pride. Women who loved proud men need a huge dose of patience, for they aren't going to come around until they're good and ready."

Jenny angled toward Moira in her seat. "I *am* being patient, but how long can this go on? He thinks of himself as flawed, and I can't seem to convince him otherwise."

"It's only natural. He sees how lovely you are and he's afraid someone will come along—some perfect man—and take you from him."

"That won't happen. I love him so much. How can I convince him?"

Moira allowed her eyes to leave the road briefly as she glanced at her niece, then shook her head. "You can't. He has to learn it himself. If he's the man for you, then one day his love for you will be stronger than his fear of others rejecting him. That's the day he'll come around for good."

Jenny sighed. "All these years I thought that if I could find someone to love who'd love me in return, there'd be no more problems."

"It's never like that Jenny, except for a rare few." Moira turned onto the coastal road leading to their house.

No, she didn't suppose it was. "I don't feel like going home. Would you mind dropping me at the cottage, please?"

"Of course not. Lovers need to be together."

How wistful she sounded, Jenny thought. How had her aunt managed to live without her lover all these years?

Her lover. The very words had her hands trembling. Memories of what it had been like to be in Blake's arms collided with desire to be in them again. And her blood began to heat.

Pulling into the drive, Moira stopped the car. "Will you be all right, or shall I wait?"

"I'll be fine," she said with more conviction than she felt. Impulsively she leaned over to kiss her aunt's cheek. "Don't wait up for me." Scooting out, she hurried through the gate and onto the back porch.

Standing there, she took a deep breath, then knocked. "Blake?" she called out. It was late afternoon. He could be napping or out on the beach for a swim.

Then she heard footsteps and he appeared on the other side of the screen. He swung the door open and stood back.

Suddenly hesitant, she walked in, her heart thumping. "I hope you don't mind that I came by."

He'd never seen her dressed up quite like this. Her black linen suit worn with a white silk blouse was classic, almost severe. Yet he could still see each subtle feminine curve. Quite simply, she took his breath away. "You're so beautiful," he said.

Jenny watched his eyes turn smoky gray. "If I am, it's because of you."

"I've missed you." He held out his arms.

On a grateful sigh she rushed into his embrace.

Henry Blanchard's low voice droned on as he read through the technical aspects of Lucius Starbuck's will. The house and its contents were to go to his beloved wife, Jocelyn. That was to be expected, Jenny thought as she shifted restlessly in the stiff-backed chair facing the attorney's desk.

There were stocks, bonds, shares in his engineering firm—all to Jocelyn. Listening, Jenny was surprised to discover her father had been a very wealthy man, something she'd given little thought to through the years. His widow would be very well off.

"Now, as to cash bequests." Henry paused dramatically, looking over the top of his half glasses at Jocelyn, Moira and Jenny seated across from him. "The first is fifty thousand dollars to Moira Ryan, along with free and clear title to the property she occupies, and his Mercedes."

"His Mercedes?" Jocelyn's voice was sharp with surprise.

"I believe you have your own Mercedes," Henry said soothingly. "One can only drive one car at a time, isn't that right, my dear?" As she sat back somewhat huffily, his eyes returned to the will.

So her father had remembered Moira for all she'd done for him, Jenny thought. Lucius had rarely spoken of his feelings, but perhaps in his heart he had harbored a few regrets. She kept her eyes straight ahead, aware of Jocelyn bristling beside her.

"The rest of the cash assets, invested in CDs and treasury bills, amount to just under five hundred thousand dollars at current market value. The sum total is bequeathed to Jennifer Starbuck."

Jocelyn's gasp was the only sound in the silent room. "That can't be right," she stated, rising from her chair. "When is that will dated?"

Stunned, Jenny just stared at both of them.

"A long while ago, Jocelyn," Henry said calmly. Shuffling the papers, he found the date. "Nearly ten years to the day."

Agitated, Jocelyn began to pace. "Lucius was planning to replace that old will, to make changes. He told me. Perhaps there's an updated version in your files."

Embarrassed as well as annoyed, Jenny glanced at Moira, who was wearing a look of revulsion as she frowned at Jocelyn.

Henry Blanchard slowly removed his glasses, set them on the polished surface of his desk and looked up at his dead friend's wife. "I've been Lucius's attorney for thirty years. There is no other will, nor had he ever mentioned to me that he was considering making changes."

"Perhaps he went to another attorney." Pausing at his desk, she snatched up the papers, frantically searching the pages for a sign. "Forgive me, Henry, but I'm going to have this checked out."

"Go right ahead. It's valid, ironclad and the last one. Be reasonable, Jocelyn. Your house and furnishings are worth more than half a million, and there's the stocks, the bonds, his company holdings."

She looked at him as if addressing a slightly backward child. "You should know that it takes a great deal of money to live today. The taxes alone are staggering. You want me to cash in the stocks and bonds, to sell my home? While she—" Jocelyn waved a manicured hand in Jenny's direction "—has very simple needs. Whatever would a childlike person like her do with half a million dollars?"

Jenny felt Moira's restraining touch on her arm as anger heated her face.

"I believe we've heard all we need to, Mr. Blanchard," Moira said, rising. "Would you be needing us for anything else?"

Looking apologetic, Henry stood. "I'll have the release forms and checks prepared. My secretary will call you when they're ready."

"Thank you. Let's go, Jenny."

Ignoring Jocelyn, Jenny stood and held out her hand. "Thank you, Mr. Blanchard."

They were in the car before she was able to roll her shoulders and release the tension. "I can't believe that woman," Jenny said, leaning back to the headrest. "A childlike person."

"She's had a shock, all right, poor dear," Moira said, maneuvering the car out into traffic. "Down to her last half million plus. Yes, I do feel sorry for her."

But Jenny was in no mood to see the humor in the situation. And she was still stunned over her inheritance. "Had you any idea that my father had so much to leave?"

"None, but then we were hardly confidants."

"I must say I'll think more kindly of him now, knowing he at least thought to make you more comfortable."

"A conscience purchase, lass. He never understood that what I did was for you, not him, so he owed me nothing. I've no need for his money, but I'll stick it in the bank before I let Jocelyn see a penny."

"I don't want his money, either." Moira was right. Lucius never understood that it was his love she wanted, not his money.

"It's different for you, lass. You're his blood and he's never given you much. You'll take it for this reason and this one alone—it'll give you independence. With independence you need dance to no one else's tune but your own."

"I thought you told me just the other day that education is the key to independence?"

"It is, but a little money in the bank won't hurt. That way no man can twist you around his finger."

Jenny swiveled in her seat to look at her aunt. "This has to do with Blake and me, doesn't it? What is it that you're trying to tell me?"

Moira took in a long breath before continuing. "Simply put, I think the two of you are a long way from settling things between you. Both partners should have equal say for a marriage to work. It's not easy for a woman to see the pitfalls in that first bloom of love."

"You think I'm too much in love to be sensible?"

Moira smiled. "Who in love is ever sensible?"

"You were. You wanted a different life than the man you loved wanted. And you were strong enough to walk away."

Sadness softened Moira's features. "Ah, but if I were given the choice again . . ."

"Then you have regrets?"

"Don't we all, lass? Just make sure yours are the kind you can live with easily."

Staring out the side window, Jenny leaned back. The tense morning had given her a great deal to think about.

Blake slipped off his shoes and sat back in his lounge chair in the den. Pleased with himself, he unfolded the paper he held and looked at it again. The deed to the acreage he'd shown Jenny last week. He'd bought the land and closed on the sale this morning. For the first time in his life he owned property.

It was to be a surprise for Jenny, one he looked forward to showing her. She had loved the area, the privacy, the site for the proposed house. Holding her in his arms as they'd stood at the top of the hill looking out to sea, he'd felt good, felt right. Next he'd have to locate an architect and get to work on plans.

Sipping from his glass of iced tea, he stretched out. His family knew nothing of his decision to remain in Florida, and Blake wasn't sure how he'd go about telling them. In the few brief notes he'd sent them in answer to their rambling, chatty letters, he'd never even mentioned Jenny, much less that he was thinking of marrying. It was anyone's guess how they'd take the news. Though Jenny would fit in anywhere, Blake couldn't picture his mother, whose favorite pastimes were golf, bridge and gardening, having much in common with his wife-to-be.

But it didn't really matter; he and Jenny would be better off left alone. They never ceased to find things to talk about, to do together. Blake had discovered that he enjoyed simple things—like reading a book or watching a television show—more if she were in the room with him.

What, he wondered, would Moira Ryan have to say about him taking her niece off to the far end of town? Maybe she'd be relieved at being free to travel places, a trip back to Ireland even. Of course, whenever Jenny wanted to visit her aunt, he would have no objection.

Her inheritance had come as a shock to all of them. However, he'd never known of anyone receiving half a million dollars and being less affected. Money had simply never mattered much to Jenny, perhaps because she'd never had to worry about it. And he'd see to it that she never would—they would live on *his* money. She could do with hers as she saw fit. So far the only thing she'd mentioned wanting was a car.

She'd forgiven him for not going to her father's funeral with her. Forgiven and understood. She'd been hurt by Jocelyn's behavior at the attorney's office but, as was her way, she'd put it out of her mind. He envied her her forgiving nature.

Glancing at his watch, Blake frowned. It was already two; she usually came by directly after noon. Picking up the phone, he dialed her home. It rang four times before he heard Jenny answer, her voice uncharacteristically faint.

"Jenny?" Blake said, sitting up taller. "Is something the matter?"

"I...yes. Blake would you come over? I need you."

Shoving the stool aside, he stood. "Are you hurt?"

"Not physically, no."

"I'm on my way." Rushing out, he hurried to his car.

He made the drive in record time and found Jenny curled up in a corner of the couch, her eyes red, her face damp. He sat down, sliding his arm around her. "What is it?"

"I was changing clothes to come to you when a man came to the door with a certified letter for me." She handed him a folded sheet.

As Blake read the notice, Jenny wiped her eyes. "I can't read some of the words, but I got the gist of it. It's a notice of a competency hearing. Jocelyn wants to have me declared incompetent."

Quickly scanning the notice, Blake felt the fury rise inside him. Jocelyn stated that her stepdaughter was illiterate, childlike and retarded. For her own good she should be institutionalized under Jocelyn's guardianship, the petition went on to suggest. Blake's fingers curled into a fist. "She won't get away with this."

"Why would she do this?" Jenny asked, too hurt to be angry.

"There's only one reason. She wants to control your money. As your court-appointed guardian, she could do that."

Sinking back into the couch, Jenny pulled her knees up. "Let her have the money, all of it. I never wanted it in the first place." Her headache was back; she rubbed above her eye. "Why would she hate me so much?"

"It's not hate, Jenny," Blake said, deliberately softening his tone. "It's greed."

"I can't believe she wants more. With the house, the stocks and bonds and business assets, she has a great deal. Isn't that enough?"

"For some people there's no such thing as enough."

"Well, I've had enough. I'm going to call Henry Blanchard in the morning and tell him to give Jocelyn the money so I never have to see her again." Jenny pulled her skirt down around her legs and rested her head on her bent knees. Even when she and Aunt Moira had moved out of her father's house, she hadn't felt this bereft.

Blake angled toward her on the couch. "No, you can't do that. You can't let her win."

"I can and I will."

"But you can prove you're not only competent but literate, intelligent and very bright."

"How? How do I prove that?"

"There are tests you can take, IQ tests, evaluations. I know Roberta can get them for us." He took her hand. "Not for the money, Jenny, but for your pride. You can't let Jocelyn get away with labeling you retarded."

Jenny shook back her hair and propped her head in her hand. "I *hate* confrontations and fighting, Blake. Just thinking about going into court, seeing Jocelyn sitting there all smug and righteous, makes my stomach turn. And it brings back all those memories when she and others called me retarded and worse. You don't know what it was like. I can't go through all that again."

"I know it might be painful. But you can do it."

Her head shot up and her eyes narrowed. "*I* can do it? *I* can face pain? What about you, Blake? I talked with Dr. Ambrose just the other day and he told me his brother called you. You need to have surgery on your leg, or you'll have a limp the rest of your life. You need to have plastic surgery on your face, too, so you can feel more comfortable about facing the world. But you don't want to go through the pain. Yet you want *me* to rush into *this*."

Blake turned away, running an exasperated hand through his hair. "It's not the same thing. Besides, I thought you said you cared about me just as I am. Were you lying?"

"No. I do love you the way you are. But you don't accept yourself. Everytime I ask you to go out in public, you find an excuse."

"You don't understand. Even with surgery I might not be all right again. It's a gamble, a painful one."

"My hearing is a gamble, as well. Jocelyn's a rich and powerful woman with a lot of important friends. I'm a young woman who's been thought to be retarded since I was seven years old. She can dredge up all those records, maybe even buy off the judge. Half a million's a lot of money, and Jocelyn has no scruples. It could go either way."

"You'd win," he said quietly. "The tests would prove how smart you are. She wouldn't stand a chance."

"*Maybe* I would win, after Jocelyn finished telling the court and the world every nasty thing she could about me. My privacy would be gone, my self-image destroyed and quite possibly my dignity. All I'd have left is a pile of money. Some sure thing." Jumping up from the couch, Jenny slipped her feet into her sandals. "I need some fresh air. I'm taking Rafferty for a run."

With a sigh Blake watched her hurry out the back door, call for her dog and head for the road.

Damn, but she was a stubborn woman. How could he make her see that he was right?

Chapter Twelve

Love made you do very strange things, Jenny decided as she closed the office door behind her and walked down the hallway to the bank of elevators. And she couldn't even blame Blake for her change of heart, for he hadn't brought up the competency hearing since that first afternoon when she received the notice.

Jenny pressed the button and stepped back. She'd worked at his house the following day, and each one after that for the past two weeks. She'd carefully rehearsed several scenarios on exactly what she'd say to him to counter each point he'd bring up. Only he hadn't. He'd been friendly, sweet and loving. Maddeningly so, never even alluding to anything controversial.

But the more she'd thought over her arguments, the weaker they'd become in her own mind. She did hate to let Jocelyn get away with something. But more importantly, she hated having people think her dimwitted. Blake had planted the seed and her sense of pride had done the rest. Some ends were worth the means to achieve, though she still dreaded the thought of appearing in court.

The doors opened and she stepped into the empty elevator, pushing the button for the main floor. She had gone to Roberta and asked her about the testing procedure to prove competency. As Blake had guessed, the therapist knew what to advise. First, Jenny would need an attorney, and Roberta had a friend she recommended highly. Having just spent an hour with her, Jenny could understand why.

Michelle Kinkaid was a widow in her forties with a diverse and busy practice in Fort Lauderdale. She worked sixteen hours a day, wore clothes with good labels and had kind eyes. Jenny had liked her on sight.

It had taken Michelle about fifteen minutes to read the papers, listen to her story, ask a few direct questions and decide to take Jenny's case. Next, she'd carefully explained that Jenny could be evaluated by a court-appointed, state-employed psychologist or pick from a list of independent certified psychologists approved by the court. Michelle recommended the latter and quickly phoned Dr. Duane Stevens, a Miami psychologist she'd worked with before on similar cases.

Time was of the essence, Michelle had explained, for the hearing date was only two weeks away and judges often became annoyed with postponements. She had gently scolded Jenny for delaying so long in seeking her aid. Jenny's appointment with Dr. Stevens was scheduled for early next week. The intensified testing would take two days and require several more to tabulate the results. Then an evaluation would be written and mailed to her attorney's office. Armed with that, and Roberta Ames's testimony if necessary, they had an excellent chance to defeat Jocelyn, Michelle had told her with a confident smile.

Leaving the building, Jenny walked toward Aunt Moira's car. She'd jumped another major hurdle over the weekend, learning to drive a stick shift. Though the gears still made her a little nervous, she slid behind the wheel. No one could imagine what it was like trying to make up for years of learning in a concentrated few months, unless they'd gone through it.

If only the tests would prove she was as intelligent as Aunt Moira swore she was and as bright as Blake insisted. Roberta had no doubts, either, but Jenny had enough for all of them. It had never been her experience that *sure things* existed.

Starting the engine, she shifted carefully. She hadn't told Blake she'd decided to take the tests. Perhaps she was afraid, or maybe superstitious. She would tell him in time. Easing up on the clutch, she pulled away from the curb.

As the date of the competency hearing neared, Jenny's nerves were stretched to the breaking point. A week before, as she was vacuuming Blake's den in the heat and humidity, she felt momentarily light-headed, then rushed to the bathroom and succumbed to a powerful wave of nausea.

When Blake returned from his swim, he found her lying on his couch with a wet cloth on her forehead. Frowning, he sat down alongside her. "What happened?"

Jenny removed the cloth and opened her eyes. "Must be something I ate."

"Maybe it's something you *didn't* eat. The last few meals we've shared, you only nibbled." He touched the back of his hand to her forehead. "You seem a little warm."

"Hard not to be in Florida in the summer." She moved to sit up, then moaned as she felt a sharp pain. Pressing her fist to her stomach, she lay back again.

"Maybe it's the flu," Blake suggested. She looked flushed and her hands were clammy.

"I don't think so. I'll be fine in a couple of minutes. I rarely get sick."

Another thought struck him. He'd been careful, but nothing worked without fail. "Could you be pregnant?"

"No."

"Are you sure?"

She didn't want to get clinical with him, but, yes, she was positive. Jenny eased into a sitting position and this time the room held still. "I think it's nerves, if you want the truth. My hearing's scheduled for next week."

Blake moved back to give her room. "So you did decide to fight it."

"Yes. I hired a lawyer Roberta knows and went to see the psychologist she recommended in Miami. The test results should be at my lawyer's office by the court date." She took a deep breath. "But I'm still worried."

Blake slipped his arm around her. "It'll go fine. You'll see."

She hadn't meant to bring this up today, but now that they were talking about her courtroom appearance, she might as well take it all the way. Worrying about this discussion was also a major cause of her nervous stomach, Jenny was certain.

Turning, she studied his face, the one she loved above all others. She noted how tan he now was and how nicely his gray eyes contrasted. And his magic mouth that could make her weak with just a touch. But she also saw the quiet determination in the tilt of his head and the stubborn slant of his chin. "Blake, I want you to come with me."

Perhaps he'd been expecting her request. She could almost see his features shift and harden in refusal.

"You don't need me with you. You need your attorney and the psychologist's report. And isn't your aunt going to be there?"

"Moira's sprained her ankle badly. She's off work, laid up at home and I told her to stay put." Her eyes swept over him slowly. His workouts had helped, but she knew his limp still pained him. And he was still hiding his face behind that useless bandage. Several times she had tried to persuade him to call Dr. Ambrose, but he'd adamantly refused. Since that was the case, he would have to learn to live with his physical limitations. "You, on the other hand, seem to be in great shape. And it's *you* I want with me." She let her words hang in the air.

A muscle in Blake's jaw twitched as he wrestled with how to explain himself, how to tell her of the panic he felt at the very thought. "Jenny, I'd do almost anything for you, but please don't ask me to go into that courtroom. I won't parade in public, even for you."

How had she known they'd come to this? Jenny brushed the hair back from her face with a shaky hand. "I've never loved anyone like I love you, Blake.

But if you can't be there with me in this—the fight you urged me not to turn away from—then maybe we don't have as much between us as I thought we did.'' Rising to her feet, struggling with a recurring wave of dizziness, Jenny straightened her clothing.

"You're not being fair. You know I love you, that I support you in this.''

She stood looking at him, heartsick. She'd been hurt before, but she hadn't known she could be hurt even more deeply. "If I can't count on you to stand by my side during the hard times, I'm not sure we belong together during the good times.''

Blake sank back into the couch. "I can't give you any more than I've already given. If that's not enough, then I'm sorry.''

Sorry. Yes, she was, too. Because she was determined not to break down in front of him, Jenny turned and hurried out the door. Then she was running through the gate and down the side of the road, her sandals slapping up puffs of dust, her vision blinded by the tears she didn't bother to brush away.

In her whole life she'd never come so close to begging someone.

Blake flopped onto the sand, breathing hard, exhausted. He lay there looking up into the sky, studying the cloud formations, trying to control his thoughts. But it was no use.

He couldn't get Jenny off his mind.

Every day since she'd run from his house, he'd worked out with his hand weights till he was sweating hard, then gone for a long, tiring swim. Wearily he'd dragged himself back to the cottage and tried to muster up an appetite only to find he had none. Several times he had eyed the whiskey bottle, but decided that particular oblivion had too high a price tag. So he'd simply gone to bed.

But not to sleep. By the first signs of daylight the sheets were tangled and damp and he'd gotten up to start the routine all over again. He knew he was physically fit enough to manage mild exercise. But he'd thrown caution to the winds and driven his body to its limits. By evening his muscles ached, his knee throbbed and his head pounded.

And still she was there, smiling at him when he opened his eyes and clearly visible behind his closed lids. If this was loving, they could keep it.

He didn't need her, he had told himself. She was trying to make him over, make him do things her way, make him prove himself. Why wasn't his love enough for her? He'd taken her into his life, opened up to her as he had to no other, bought land so he could build and live with her for all time. Why the hell did he have to do even more?

Sitting up with no small effort, Blake rested his arms on his bent knees and stared out to sea. For a while there she'd fooled him into believing that he could live a normal life like everyone else, that they could be happy together. She had said she would love to live in the private spot he'd picked out, that she wouldn't push him to endure the pain of the knife again, that she loved him just the way he was. Then, the first time he refused to do her bidding, she turned from him.

He watched a gull circle overhead. Well, maybe not the first time. But she had no right demanding that he go places with her when she knew he hated the way people stared at him. Sure, he had nagged her into going to see Roberta Ames, but that had been for her own good. And it had worked out. But she was nagging him to do something that would doom him to possibly a whole year of suffering, maybe longer. And might *not* work out.

There was no question in his mind, Blake thought as he struggled to his feet. Jenny Starbuck was a stubborn Irishwoman, single-minded in her desire to push him toward pain, with not a thought about his own feelings.

And he loved her beyond all reason.

Walking slowly back to the cottage, he saw some of his clothes he hadn't bothered to take down still flapping on the clothesline where Jenny had hung them. His mind traveled back to the days he had watched her hang washing, humming a tune, laughing and romping with Rafferty. And he saw again the look of pure joy on her face when she finished reading to him that first time. Then his chest tightened as he remembered how she had looked in his bed that night of the storm, her lovely hair spread out on the pillow, her eyes widening with pleasure as he'd filled her.

He'd been hurt when Eleanor had shown him she didn't care enough to stay with him. But he'd come to realize her rejection had hurt his pride more than his heart. This was different. Jenny's running from him had twisted the knife, even though it had been his words that had sent her away.

Inside the cottage Blake limped to the bathroom and gazed at his own reflection. The man who stared back at him with hollow eyes needed a shave, a shower and a good night's sleep. The problem was, he wasn't apt to get the latter until he straightened out his life. And the only way to do that was to go to Jenny and confess a terrible truth: that without her in his life, he simply didn't give a damn about much.

Reaching for his razor, he realized that tomorrow was to be her day in court. He would go to her today, right after cleaning up, and tell her what he had learned. And hope that her forgiving heart hadn't run out of patience.

Frowning, Blake began to shave.

Rafferty greeted him exuberantly, as always, as he climbed onto Jenny's back porch. He ruffled the dog's shaggy head, then knocked twice. There were no signs of anyone moving around. Of course, it was possible she was out, perhaps working for Dr. Swain. He knocked again, harder.

"Hold on, I'm coming." Moira's voice was impatient, her accent heavier than usual. Shifting her weight to one foot, she unlocked the door for him. "So it's you," she muttered as she hobbled back into the living room.

"Looks like we could both use a cane," Blake said, following her in. "Jenny told me you'd sprained your ankle."

Moira eased herself back into her chair with a heavy sigh. "Aye, and what a bother it is."

She was fully dressed in a plain suit and no-nonsense blouse, though shoeless. He wondered why she was going out with such a swollen ankle. "Yes, I'm familiar with leg injuries." He glanced around. "Is Jenny at home?"

"No, she's in court. Sit yourself down, Major. It hurts my neck to keep looking up at you."

Blake sat on the edge of the couch. "I thought the court date was for tomorrow."

"It was, but there was some mix-up on the docket, or so Jenny was told. Her attorney called yesterday and told her to be there this morning at nine sharp."

Blake fidgeted, wondering how much Moira Ryan knew. "I thought I might talk with her, tell her I support her decision. That sort of thing."

"Is that a fact? A mite tardy with your support, aren't you, Major?" Moira removed her glasses and began polishing them.

Odd how this small woman could make him squirm. Blake cleared his throat. "I told Jenny a long while back that I was all for her standing up to her stepmother and fighting this competency ruling. I even advised that she go to Roberta Ames and—"

"I don't give a fig about all that. The truth is, she needed you by her side and you let her down."

Blake got to his feet. He didn't have to listen to this. "I'm sorry you feel that way. I believe Jenny will listen to me and realize that—"

"Bullheaded is what you are. Just like Lucius Starbuck."

Shoving his hands into his pockets, Blake glared at her. "I'm not a bit like her father."

"Aren't you, though? Didn't you abandon her, too, when she needed you? Don't your reasons center around keeping yourself happy at her expense, just like his did?" Replacing her glasses, Moira peered up at him.

Blake spoke through clenched teeth. "It's not the same."

"No, that it isn't. Jenny was always a bit frightened of her father. Ah, but she rushed to you with open arms. And she gave her heart to you, which is more than she's done before. There've been other men who've wanted her, you know. Don't think there haven't. But she turned away from each one until you. I'm thinking her judgment of men is no better than mine was at her age. More's the pity.''

Blake sat back down and leaned forward, wanting inexplicably to explain himself to this woman. ''You're wrong. I love Jenny. I want to marry her. I've even bought some land for a home.''

''Aye, she told me. I know the place, up past town in the middle of nowhere. You want to shut Jenny away in that hilltop house you plan to build. You think if you hide her from other men's eyes, she'll stay with you. But you can't keep her that way, Major, not any more than you can tame that wild cat she took into your home. You can't hold a woman or an animal unless they want to be held.''

It'd been a long while since he'd been so neatly put in his place, if ever. Giving himself a moment, he watched her put on her shoes, grimacing at the discomfort. She was quite a lady. ''You love her very much, don't you?''

''Aye, and it pains me to see her hurting the way she is. There's been no laughter in this house for a week now, and she hasn't eaten enough to keep a bird alive. There's no denying I'm angry with you for bringing her to that, you who claim to love her.'' At last, shoes on, she sighed noisily.

''What can I do to make it up to her?''

''You'll think of something, if you care enough.'' Carefully Moira pushed to her feet. ''Now, if you'll excuse me, I've got to take these papers over to the courthouse.''

''To Jenny? What papers?''

"From the beginning there's been one thing, then another going wrong on this dreadful hearing. The change of date and now this." She picked up an envelope from the table. "Jenny's test results. They were supposed to have been sent to her attorney, but that Miami doctor's careless secretary sent them here. Michelle Kinkaid told Jenny to take them along this morning, but the poor lass was so troubled, she forgot them. Michelle phoned a bit ago and asked if I could get them to her quickly. Otherwise they'll have to request a postponement. I can't watch Jenny go through the agony of waiting another day."

He had his answer. It had been in front of him all along, but he'd been too stubborn to see. Blake held out his hand. "I really think you should rest. I'll take that to Jenny."

Moira stared up at him for a long moment, then her eyes behind her glasses flashed approval as she sat back down. "I think there's hope for you, Major."

Smiling, he bent and kissed her cheek. "One question. Did you read her report?"

"Aye, we both did. She scored a 138, definitely on the high end of the intelligence curve."

"I knew it." He slipped the envelope into his pocket. "Thank you, Moira. I haven't been taken to task so well since I was about eight years old."

"Perhaps you were overdue. Now I've a favor to ask."

"Ask away."

"Would you take off that silly bandage?"

He hesitated only for a moment, then pulled it off.

Moira smiled. "One more thing. They reconvene at two, so you'll have time."

"Time for what?"

"To stop at the cottage and slip on your uniform."
Her eyes lit up. "Ah, Major, there's something about
a man in uniform that makes a woman's heart speed
up."

Blake leaned down to grip her hand. "You're a
wicked woman, Moira Ryan."

"And you, Blake Hanley, are a sight for sore eyes.
Go rescue your fair maiden."

Hardly limping at all, Blake hurried to his car.

Her hands were damp, her legs trembled and the
butterflies in her stomach had definitely multiplied.
Jenny sat staring straight ahead at the judge, a bald-
ing man with a graying beard and bored eyes. He
seemed to be hardly listening as Jocelyn Starbuck's
attorney presented her petition, offering as evidence a
respectable accumulation of paperwork compiled on
Jenny's learning disabilities as a child. She tried very
hard to concentrate on the oak graining of the judge's
bench rather than on the painful words.

Because the doctor's report had been misdirected,
Jocelyn's attorney hadn't seen Jenny's test results.
However, even knowing what they were, Jenny was
nervous. So much could go wrong. The judge had
smiled warmly at Jocelyn as they'd begun, looking for
all the world like an old friend. Fighting anxiety, she
looked over her shoulder at the double doors leading
into the courtroom. Ten after two. Where was Aunt
Moira?

Michelle Kinkaid touched Jenny's arm and leaned
close to her ear. "Your aunt will be here momentarily. She assured me she'd hurry. When it's our turn, I
can drag Roberta's testimony out until Moira gets
here. Relax, Jenny."

Jenny nodded her thanks, then resumed shredding the tissue in her fingers. How stupid she'd been to forget the most important part of her defense. It was just that she'd been so upset by all this that she hadn't slept much, hadn't been thinking clearly. The occasional headache had turned into a constant throbbing. Perhaps after today things would return to normal.

Normal. What was that? She could never return to the way things were before Blake had entered her life. She'd forever left behind that simple time. Diagnosing her dyslexia had changed everything, opened new worlds to her. Being able to drive alone had freed her. She could go on to college now. She'd have the money for tuition, provided she won this case. But there still remained one big problem.

None of it held any appeal if Blake wasn't with her.

Shutting out the voices around her, she concentrated on Blake. Perhaps she had been better off before she'd known what it was like to love him. No, as painful as it was losing him, she didn't regret the time they'd shared.

He was such a beautiful man. Why couldn't he see? She remembered his silly grin when she spotted the tennis shoe on the end of her fishing pole. Then there was his gentleness when she had cleaned the injured cat, even though Mr. No-nose had hissed at him fiercely. And the comfort, the strength she'd found as he'd held her after she told him she couldn't read.

He would probably go back to Michigan now, and one day would finally realize how very special he was. She hoped it would happen soon. She had tried, but been unable to... Hearing the doors open at the rear, she swung about.

Major Blake Hanley paused just inside the court-room, tall and handsome in his crisp uniform, his stance confident. Then he walked down the center aisle toward Jenny, his back straight, his limp barely visible, his eyes never wavering as he smiled at her. His face was clean-shaven and bandage-free. Jenny choked back a sob as she watched him lean down to Michelle and hand her an envelope.

"Jenny's test results," he whispered. "Would it be possible for me to sit in that chair alongside her?"

One glance at Jenny's face had Michelle nodding, then she opened the envelope to study the psychologist's report.

Across the aisle Jocelyn stared at the newcomer with ill-disguised curiosity. As her attorney sat down, she grabbed at his sleeve and whispered to him.

But Jenny had eyes only for Blake. She had never seen him in uniform before. He took her breath away.

Slipping quietly into the chair next to Jenny, Blake reached for her hand. She wore a simple black dress, her eyes were huge in her pale face. Then she smiled, not bothering to hide her love for him, and his heart soared. His fingers tightening in hers, he leaned close to her ear. "I love you."

It was all Jenny could do to keep from kissing him right there in the courtroom. It was going to be all right, she thought as she blinked back the sudden moisture from her eyes. Blake was here with her, and everything was going to be all right.

She swung her eyes back to the front, anxious to get on with the proceedings.

It was early dawn and they were walking barefoot on the beach, hands intertwined. The sky was just beginning to lighten and a few night stars hadn't disappeared yet. Shirtless and with his white pants rolled halfway up his legs, Blake turned to look at Jenny. He was absolutely certain he would never tire of looking at Jenny.

She wore the somewhat shapeless blue dress he'd first seen her in, and her long hair shifted in the breeze. Her eyes were filled with laughter as she gazed up at him.

"I can't get over the look on Jocelyn's face when Michelle introduced the test results," she said with a chuckle. "She all but snatched the papers from her attorney's hands the moment he got them."

Blake's arm went around her, drawing her close to his side. "And didn't she look stunned when she accused you of going to some quack for the tests and the judge informed her that Dr. Stevens was probably the most highly respected psychologist in the state of Florida."

Jenny laughed out loud. "I loved it! Poor Jocelyn. As Aunt Moira said, she'll have to struggle along on her stocks and bonds and other assets."

"She could sell the family manse."

Kicking happily at the sand, she shook her head. "Not and still hold her head up high in Fort Lauderdale society. Which is slightly more important to Jocelyn than breathing." She stopped then, her face growing serious. "You know, I feel sorry for her. All she's got is money."

Blake pulled her into the circle of his arms. "I've never been against having money. But I found out recently that it means very little if you haven't got the person you love."

Jenny slid her hands up his chest and linked them behind his neck. "Tell me again."

"I love you, Jenny Starbuck."

"I don't think I'll ever get tired of hearing it." She kissed him, gently at first, then with rising passion. They'd just come from his big bed and a long night of loving, yet she wanted him again. "Mmm, maybe it's time to head back to a more private place."

"Good idea. I think we ought to spend the next whole week in bed because we won't be able to sleep together for a while after Saturday."

"What happens Saturday?"

His face was shadowed, serious. "I've booked us on a flight to San Antonio. I'm checking into Brooks Medical Center for surgery on my leg, and I thought you might want to come with me."

Jenny searched his eyes. "If you're doing this for me..."

His arms tightened around her. "I'm doing this for me, for you *and* for our children. Who wants a father who's grumpy all the time because he's in pain? After that, well, we'll talk about plastic surgery."

Tenderly she framed his face with loving hands. "I know that was a difficult decision. I'm proud of you."

"I couldn't have made it without you. I want you to be proud of me."

"I *am* proud of you. I always have been. A woman looks at her man through the eyes of love and sees only perfection. Didn't you know that?"

Instead of answering, he kissed her, long and hard. "About that private spot..."

Jenny laughed and grabbed his hand. As she turned, she glanced up at the sky. "Oh, look! The morning star, still shining brightly."

He looked up. "It fools us all with its persistent beauty." Blake shifted his eyes to Jenny's. "Like you did."

Smiling, she tugged at him. "Come on. Let's go home."

* * * * *

NORA ROBERTS

Love has a language all its own, and for centuries, flowers have symbolized love's finest expression. Discover the language of flowers—and love—in this romantic collection of 48 favorite books by bestselling author Nora Roberts.

Starting in February, two titles will be available each month at your favorite retail outlet.

In March, look for:

Irish Rose, Volume #3
Storm Warning, Volume #4

In April, look for:

First Impressions, Volume #5
Reflections, Volume #6

Collect all 48 titles and become fluent in

THE LANGUAGE of LOVE

LOL392

Silhouette Special Edition

salutes

MOMENTS OF GLORY

from Lindsay McKenna

In a country torn with conflict, in a time of bitter passions, these brave men and women wage a war against all odds . . . and a timeless battle for honor, for fleeting moments of glory, for the promise of enduring love.

February: RIDE THE TIGER (#721) Survivor Dany Villard is wise to the love-'em-and-leave-'em ways of war, but wounded hero Gib Ramsey swears she's captured his heart . . . forever.

March: ONE MAN'S WAR (#727) The war raging inside brash and bold Captain Pete Mallory threatens to destroy him, until Tess Ramsey's tender love guides him toward peace.

April: OFF LIMITS (#733) Soft-spoken Marine Jim McKenzie saved Alexandra Vance's life in Vietnam; now he needs her love to save his honor. . . .

Take 4 bestselling love stories FREE

Plus get a FREE surprise gift!

From the popular author of the bestselling title
DUNCAN'S BRIDE (Intimate Moments #349)
comes the

LINDA HOWARD

COLLECTION

Two exquisite collector's editions that contain four of
Linda Howard's early passionate love stories. To add
these special volumes to your own library, be sure
to look for:

VOLUME ONE: *Midnight Rainbow*
                  Diamond Bay
                  (Available in March)

VOLUME TWO: *Heartbreaker*
                  White Lies
                  (Available in April)

Silhouette Books®

SLH92